Wet Magic

Wet Magic

By

E. Nesbit

With illustrations by

H.R. Millar

NEW YORK

Books of Wonder

1996

TO

Dr. E. N. da C. Andrade

from

E. Nesbit

Well Hall
Kent

First published by Macmillan & Co. 1913

First published in this edition 1996 by
Books of Wonder
16 West 18th Street
New York, NY 10011

Design and typography © 1996 by Ozma, Inc.

Printed in the U.S.A.

ISBN 0-929605-63-2 (hardcover)

ISBN 0-929605-54-3 (paperback)

1 2 3 4 5 6 7 8 9

List of Chapters

Wet Magic

Sabrina Fair

That going to the seaside was the very beginning of everything — only it seemed as though it were going to be a
beginning without an end, like the roads on the Sussex downs
which look like roads and then look like paths, and then turn
into sheep tracks, and then are just grass and furze bushes and
tottergrass and harebells and rabbits and chalk.

The children had been counting the days to The Day.
Bernard indeed had made a calendar on a piece of cardboard
that had once been the bottom of the box in which his new white
sandshoes came home. He marked the divisions of the weeks
quite neatly in red ink, and the days were numbered in blue ink,
and every day he crossed off one of those numbers with a piece
of green chalk he happened to have left out of a penny box.
Mavis had washed and ironed all the dolls' clothes at least a
fortnight before The Day. This was thoughtful and farsighted of
her, of course, but it was a little trying to Kathleen, who was
much younger and who would have preferred to go on playing
with her dolls in their dirtier and more familiar state.

"Well, if you do," said Mavis, a little hot and cross from the
ironing board, "I'll never wash anything for you again, not even
your face."

Kathleen somehow felt as if she could bear that.

"But mayn't I have just one of the dolls" was, however, all she said, — "just the teeniest, weeniest one? Let me have Lord Edward. His head's half gone as it is, and I could dress him in a clean hanky and pretend it was kilts."

Mavis could not object to this, because, of course, whatever else she washed she didn't wash hankies. So Lord Edward had his pale kilts, and the other dolls were put away in a row in Mavis's corner drawer. It was after that that Mavis and Francis had long secret consultations, — and when the younger ones asked questions they were told, "It's secrets. You'll know in good time." This, of course, excited everyone very much indeed — and it was rather a comedown when the good time came, and the secret proved to be nothing more interesting than a large empty aquarium which the two elders had clubbed their money together to buy, for eight and nine pence in the Old Kent Road. They staggered up the front garden path with it, very hot and tired.

"But what are you going to do with it?" Kathleen asked, as they all stood around the nursery table looking at it.

"Fill it with seawater," Francis explained, "to put sea anemones in.

"Oh yes," said Kathleen with enthusiasm, — "and the crabs and starfish and prawns and the yellow periwinkles — and all the common objects of the seashore."

"We'll stand it in the window," Mavis added: "it'll make the lodgings look so distinguished."

"And then perhaps some great scientific gentleman, like Darwin or Faraday, will see it as he goes by, and it will be such a joyous surprise to him to come face-to-face with our jellyfish; he'll offer to teach Francis all about science for nothing — *I* see," said Kathleen hopefully.

"But how will you get it to the seaside?" Bernard asked, leaning his hands on the schoolroom table and breathing heavily into the aquarium, so that its shining sides became dim and misty. "It's much too big to go in the boxes, you know."

"Then I'll carry it," said Francis, "it won't be in the way at all — I carried it home today."

"We had to take the bus, you know," said truthful Mavis, "and then I had to help you."

"I don't believe they'll let you take it at all," said Bernard — if you know anything of grown-ups you will know that Bernard proved to be quite right.

"Take an aquarium to the seaside — nonsense!" they said. And "What for?" not waiting for the answer. "They," just at present, was Aunt Enid.

Francis had always been passionately fond of water. Even when he was a baby he always stopped crying the moment they put him in the bath. And he was the little boy who, at the age of four, was lost for three hours and then brought home by the police who had found him sitting in a horse trough in front of the Willing Mind, wet to the topmost hair of his head, and quite happy, entertaining a circle of carters with pots of beer in their hands. There was very little water in the horse trough and the most talkative of the carters explained that, the kid being that wet at the first start off, him and his mates thought he was as safe in the trough as anywhere — the weather being what it was and all them nasty motors and trams about.

To Francis, passionately attracted as he was by water in all forms, from the simple mud puddle to the complicated machinery by which your bath supply is enabled to get out of order, it was a real tragedy that he had never seen the sea. Something had always happened to prevent it. Holidays had been spent in green countries where there were rivers and wells and ponds, and waters deep and wide — but the water had been fresh water, and the green grass had been on each side of it. One great charm of the sea, as he had heard of it, was that it had nothing on the other side "so far as eye could see." There was a lot about the sea in poetry, and Francis, curiously enough, liked poetry.

The buying of the aquarium had been an attempt to make sure that, having found the sea, he should not lose it again. He imagined the aquarium fitted with a real rock in the middle, to which radiant sea anemones clung and limpets stuck. There were to be yellow periwinkles too, and seaweeds, and gold and silver fish (which don't live in the sea by the way, only Francis didn't know this), flitting about in radiant scaly splendor, among the shadows of the growing water plants. He had thought it all out — how a cover might be made, very light, with rubber in between, like a screw-top bottle, to keep the water in while it traveled home in the guard's van to the admiration of passengers and porters at both stations. And now — he was not to be allowed to take it.

He told Mavis, and she agreed with him that it was a shame.

"But I'll tell you what," she said, for she was not one of those comforters who just say, "I'm sorry," and don't try to help. She generally thought of something that would make things at any rate just a little better. "Let's fill it with fresh water, and get some goldfish and sand and weeds; and I'll make Eliza promise to put ants' eggs in — that's what they eat — and it'll be something to break the dreadful shock when we have to leave the sea and come home again."

Francis admitted that there was something in this and consented to fill the aquarium with water from the bath. When this was done the aquarium was so heavy that the combined efforts of all four children could not begin to move it.

"Never mind," said Mavis, the consoler; "let's empty it out again and take it back to the common room, and then fill it by secret jugfuls, carried separately, you know."

This might have been successful, but Aunt Enid met the first secret jugful — and forbade the second.

"Messing about," she called it. "No, of course I shan't allow you to waste your money on fish." And Mother was already at the seaside getting the lodgings ready for them. Her last words had been —

"Be sure you do exactly what Aunt Enid says." So, of course, they had to. Also Mother had said, "Don't argue," — so they had not even the melancholy satisfaction of telling Aunt Enid that she was quite wrong, and that they were not messing about at all.

Aunt Enid was not a real aunt, but just an old friend of Grandmamma's, with an aunt's name and privileges and rather more than an aunt's authority. She was much older than a real aunt and not half so nice. She was what is called "firm" with children, and no one ever called her auntie. Just Aunt Enid. That will tell you in a moment.

So there the aquarium was, dishearteningly dry — for even the few drops left in it from its first filling dried up almost at once.

Even in its unwatery state, however, the aquarium was beautiful. It had not any of that ugly ironwork with red lead showing between the iron and the glass which you may some-times have noticed in the aquariums of your friends. No, it was one solid thick piece of clear glass, faintly green, and when you stooped down and looked through you could almost fancy that there really was water in it.

"Let's put flowers in it," Kathleen suggested, "and pretend they're anemones. Do let's, Francis."

"I don't care what you do," said Francis. "I'm going to read *The Water Babies*."

"Then we'll do it, and make it a lovely surprise for you," said Kathleen cheerily.

Francis sat down squarely with *The Water Babies* flat before him on the table, where also his elbows were, and the others, respecting his sorrow, stole quietly away. Mavis just stepped back to say, "I say, France, you don't mind their putting flowers? It's to please you, you know."

"I tell you I don't mind *anything*," said Francis savagely.

When the three had finished with it, the aquarium really looked rather nice, and, if you stooped down and looked sideways through the glass, like a real aquarium.

Kathleen took some clinkers from the back of the rockery — "where they won't show," she said — and Mavis induced these to stand up like an arch in the middle of the glassy square. Tufts of long grass, rather sparingly arranged, looked not unlike waterweed. Bernard begged from the cook some of the fine silver sand which she uses to scrub the kitchen tables and dressers with, and Mavis cut the thread of the Australian shell necklace that Uncle Robert sent her last Christmas, so that there should be real, shimmery, silvery shells on the sand. (This was rather self-sacrificing of her, because she knew she would have to put them all back again on their string, and you know what a bother shells are to thread.) They shone delightfully through the glass. But the great triumph was the sea anemones — pink and red and yellow — clinging to the rocky arch just as though they were growing there.

"Oh, lovely, lovely," Kathleen cried, as Mavis fixed the last delicate flesh-tinted crown. "Come and look, France."

"Not yet," said Mavis, in a great hurry, and she tied the thread of the necklace round a tin goldfish (out of the box with the duck and the boat and the mackerel and the lobster and the magnet that makes them all move about — you know) and hung it from the middle of the arch. It looked just as though it were swimming — you hardly noticed the thread at all.

"*Now*, France," she called. And Francis came slowly with his thumb in *The Water Babies*. It was nearly dark by now, but Mavis had lighted the four dollhouse candles in the gilt candlesticks and set them on the table around the aquarium.

"Look through the side," she said; "isn't it ripping?"

"Why," said Francis slowly, "you've got water in it — and real anemones! Where on earth...?"

"Not real," said Mavis. "I wish they were; they're only dahlias. But it does look pretty, doesn't it?"

"It's like Fairyland," said Kathleen, and Bernard added, "I *am* glad you bought it."

"It just shows what it will be like when we *do* get the sea creatures," said Mavis. "Oh, Francis, you do like it, don't you?"

"Oh, I like it all right," he answered, pressing his nose against the thick glass, "but I wanted it to be waving weeds and mysterious wetness like the Sabrina picture."

The other three glanced at the picture which hung over the mantelpiece — Sabrina and the water nymphs, drifting along among the waterweeds and water lilies. There were words under the picture, and Francis dreamily began to say them:

"Sabrina fair
    Listen where thou art sitting,
Under the glassie, cool, translucent wave'
    In twisted braids of Lillies knitting
The loose train of thy amber-dropping hair..."

"Hullo — what was that?" he said in quite a different voice, and jumped up.

"What was what?" the others naturally asked.

"Did you put something alive in there?" Francis asked.

"Of course not," said Mavis. "Why?"

"Well, I saw something move, that's all." They all crowded around and peered over the glass walls. Nothing, of course, but the sand and the grass and the shells, the clinkers and the dahlias and the little suspended tin goldfish.

"I expect the goldfish swung a bit," said Bernard. "That's what it must have been."

"It didn't look like that," Francis answered. "It looked more like — "

"Like what?"

"I don't know — get out of the light. Let's have another squint."

He stooped down and looked again through the glass.

"It's not the goldfish," he said. "That's as quiet as a trout asleep. No — I suppose it was a shadow or something."

"You might tell us what it looked like," said Kathleen.

"Was it like a rat?" Bernard asked with interest.

"Not a bit. It was more like — "

"Well, like what?" asked three aggravated voices.

"Like Sabrina — only very, very tiny."

"A sort of doll — Sabrina," said Kathleen, "how awfully jolly!"

"It wasn't at all like a doll, and it wasn't jolly," said Francis shortly — "only I wish it would come again."

It didn't, however.

"I say," said Mavis, struck by a new idea, "perhaps it's a magic aquarium."

"Let's play it is," suggested Kathleen — "let's play it's a magic glass and we can see what we like in it. I see a fairy palace with gleaming spires of crystal and silver."

"I see a football match, and our chaps winning," said Bernard heavily, joining in the new game.

"Shut up," said Francis. "That isn't play. There *was* something."

"Suppose it is magic," said Mavis again.

"We've played magic so often, and nothing's ever happened — even when we made the fire of sweet-scented woods and eastern gums, and all that," said Bernard. "it's much better to pretend right away. We always have to in the end. Magic just wastes time. There isn't any magic really, is there, Mavis?"

"Shut up, I tell you," was the only answer of Francis, his nose now once more flattened against the smooth green glass.

Here Aunt Enid's voice was heard on the landing outside, saying, "Little ones — bed," in no uncertain tones.

The two grunted as it were in whispers, but there was no appeal against Aunt Enid, and they went, their grunts growing feebler as they crossed the room, and dying away in a despairing silence as they and Aunt Enid met abruptly at the top of the stairs.

"Shut the door," said Francis, in a strained sort of voice. And Mavis obeyed, even though he hadn't said "please." She really was an excellent sister. Francis, in moments of weakness, had gone so far as to admit that she wasn't half bad.

"I say," she said when the click of the latch assured her that they were alone, "how could it be magic? We never said any spell."

"No more we did," said Francis, "unless — And besides, it's all nonsense, of course, about magic. It's just a game we play, isn't it?"

"Yes, of course," Mavis said doubtfully; "but what did you mean by 'unless'?"

"We weren't saying any spells, were we?"

"No, of course we weren't — we weren't saying anything—"

"As it happens *I* was."

"Was what? When?"

"When it happened."

"What happened?"

Will it be believed that Aunt Enid chose this moment for opening the door just wide enough to say, "Mavis — bed." And

Mavis had to go. But as she went she said again: "*What happened?*"

"*It*," said Francis, "whatever it was. I was saying..."

"*MAVIS!*" called Aunt Enid.

"Yes, Aunt Enid — you were saying *what?*"

"I was saying, *Sabrina fair*," said Francis, "do you think — but, of course, it couldn't have been — and all dry like that, no water or anything."

"Perhaps magic *has* to be dry," said Mavis. "Coming, Aunt Enid! It seems to be mostly burning things, and, of course, that wouldn't do in the water. What *did* you see?"

"It looked like Sabrina," said Francis — "only tiny, tiny. Not doll-small, you know, but live-small, like through the wrong end of a telescope. I do wish you'd seen it."

"Say, 'Sabrina fair' again quick while I look."

"Sabrina fair
    Listen where thou art sitting
Under the —

"Oh, Mavis, it is — it did. There's something there truly. Look!"

"Where?" said Mavis. "I can't see — oh, let me look."

"*MAVIS!*" called Aunt Enid very loud indeed; and Mavis tore herself away.

"I must go," she said. "Never mind, we'll look again tomorrow. Oh, France, if it *should* be — magic, I mean — I'll tell you what — "

But she never told him what, for Aunt Enid swept in and swept out, bearing Mavis away, as it were, in a whirlwind of impatient exasperation, and, without seeming to stop to do it, blowing out the four candles as she came and went.

At the door she turned to say, "Good night, Francis. Your bath's turned on ready. Be sure you wash well behind your ears. We shan't have much time in the morning.

"But Mavis always bathes first," said he. "I'm the eldest."

"Don't argue, child, for goodness' sake," said Aunt Enid. "Mavis is having the flat bath in my bedroom to save time. Come — no nonsense," she paused at the door to say. "Let me see you go. Right about face — quick march!"

And he had to.

"If she must pretend to give orders like drill, she might at least learn to say *Bout turn!*" he reflected, struggling with his collar stud in the steaming bathroom. "Never mind. I'll get up early and see if I can't see it again."

And so he did — but early as he was, Aunt Enid and the servants were earlier. The aquarium was empty — clear, clean, shining and quite empty.

Aunt Enid could not understand why Francis ate so little breakfast.

"What has she done with them?" he wondered later.

"*I* know," said Bernard solemnly. "She told Esther to put them on the kitchen fire — I only just saved my fish."

"And what about my shells?" asked Mavis in sudden fear.

"Oh, she took those to take care of. Said you weren't old enough to take care of them yourself."

You will wonder why the children did not ask their Aunt Enid right out what had become of the contents of the aquarium. Well, you don't know their Aunt Enid. And besides, even on that first morning, before anything that really *was* anything could be said to have happened — for, after all, what Francis said he had seen might have been just fancy — there was a sort of misty, curious, trembling feeling at the hearts of Mavis and her brother which made them feel that they did not want to talk about the aquarium and what had been in it to any grown-up — and least of all to their Aunt Enid.

And leaving the aquarium, that was the hardest thing of all. They thought of telegraphing to Mother, to ask whether, after all, they mightn't bring it — but there was first the difficulty of wording a telegram so that their mother would understand and not deem it insanity or a practical joke — secondly, the fact that ten pence half-penny, which was all they had between them, would not cover the baldest statement of the facts.

MRS DESMOND,
    CARE OF MRS PEARCE,
      EAST CLIFF VILLA,
        LEWIS ROAD,
          WEST BEACHFIELD-ON-SEA, SUSSEX

alone would be eight pence — and the simplest appeal, such as "May we bring aquarium please say yes wire reply" brought the whole thing hopelessly beyond their means.

"It's no good," said Francis hopelessly. "And, anyway," said Kathleen, "there wouldn't be time to get an answer before we go."

No one had thought of this. It was a sort of backhanded consolation.

"But think of coming back to it," said Mavis, "it'll be something to live for, when we come back from the sea and everything else is beastly."

And it was.

The Captive

The delicate pinkish bloom of newness was on the wooden spades, the slick smoothness of the painted pails showed neither scratch nor dent on their green and scarlet surface — the shrimping nets were full and fluffy as, once they and sand and water had met, they never could be again. The pails and spades and nets formed the topmost layer of a pile of luggage — you know the sort of thing, with the big boxes at the bottom; and the carryall bulging with its wraps and mackers; the old portmanteau that shows its striped lining through the crack and is so useful for putting boots in; and the sponge bag, and all the little things that get left out. You can almost always squeeze a ball or a paint box or a box of chalks or any of those things — which grown-ups say you won't really want till you come back — into that old portmanteau — and then when it's being unpacked at the journey's end the most that can happen will be that someone will say, "I thought I told you not to bring that," and if you don't answer back, that will be all. But most likely in the agitation of unpacking and settling in, your tennis ball, or pencil box, or whatever it is, will pass unnoticed. Of course, you can't shove an aquarium into the old portmanteau — nor a pair of rabbits, nor a hedgehog — but anything in reason you can.

The luggage that goes in the van is not much trouble — of course, it has to be packed and to be strapped, and labeled and looked after at the junction, but apart from that the big luggage behaves itself, keeps itself to itself, and like your elder brothers at college never occasions its friends a moment's anxiety. It is the younger fry of the luggage family, the things you have with you in the carriage that are troublesome — the bundle of umbrellas and walking sticks, the golf clubs, the rugs, the greatcoats, the basket of things to eat, the books you are going to read in the train and as often as not you never look at them, the newspapers that the grown-ups are tired of and yet don't want to throw away, their little bags or dispatch cases and suit-cases and card cases, and scarfs and gloves —

The children were traveling under the care of Aunt Enid, who always had far more of these tiresome odds and ends than Mother had — and it was at the last moment, when the cab was almost to be expected to be there, that Aunt Enid rushed out to the corner shop and returned with four new spades, four new pails, and four new shrimping nets, and presented them to the children just in time for them to be added to the heap of odds and ends with which the cab was filled up.

"I hope it's not ungrateful," said Mavis at the station as they stood waiting by the luggage mound while Aunt Enid went to take the tickets — "but why couldn't she have bought them at Beachfield?"

"Makes us look such babies," said Francis, who would not be above using a wooden spade at the proper time and place but did not care to be branded in the face of all Waterloo Junction as one of those kids off to the seaside with little spades and pails.

Kathleen and Bernard were, however, young enough to derive a certain pleasure from stroking the smooth, curved surface of the spades till Aunt Enid came fussing back with the tickets and told them to put their gloves on for goodness' sake and try not to look like street children.

I am sorry that the first thing you should hear about the children should be that they did not care about their Aunt Enid, but this was unfortunately the case. And if you think this was not nice of them I can only remind you that you do not know their Aunt Enid.

There was a short, sharp struggle with the porter, a flustered passage along the platform and the children were safe in the carriage marked "Reserved" — thrown into it, as it were, with all that small fry of luggage which I have just described. Then Aunt Enid fussed off again to exchange a few last home truths with the porter, and the children were left.

"We breathe again," said Mavis.

"Not yet we don't," said Francis, "there'll be some more fuss as soon as she comes back. I'd almost as soon not go to the sea as go with her."

"But you've never seen the sea," Mavis reminded him.

"I know," said Francis, morosely, "but look at all this — " he indicated the tangle of their possessions which littered seats and rack — "I do wish — "

He stopped, for a head appeared in the open doorway — in a round hat very like Aunt Enid's — but it was not Aunt Enid's. The face under the hat was a much younger, kinder one.

"I'm afraid this carriage is reserved," said the voice that belonged to the face.

"Yes," said Kathleen, "but there's lots of room if you like to come too."

"I don't know if the aunt we're with would like it," said the more cautious Mavis. "*We* should, of course," she added to meet the kind smiling eyes that looked from under the hat that was like Aunt Enid's.

The lady said: "I'm an aunt too — I'm going to meet my nephew at the junction. The train's frightfully crowded... If I were to talk to your aunt... perhaps on the strength of our common aunthood. The train will start in a minute. I haven't any luggage to be a bother — nothing but one paper." — she had indeed a folded newspaper in her hands.

"Oh, do get in," said Kathleen, dancing with anxiety, "I'm sure Aunt Enid won't mind," — Kathleen was always hopeful — "suppose the train were to start or anything!"

"Well, if you think I may," said the lady, and tossed her paper into the corner in a lighthearted way which the children found charming. Her pleasant face was rising in the oblong of the carriage doorway, her foot was on the carriage step, when suddenly she retreated back and down. It was almost as though someone pulled her off the carriage step.

"Excuse me," said a voice, "this carriage is reserved." The pleasant face of the lady disappeared and the — well, the face of Aunt Enid took its place. The lady vanished. Aunt Enid trod on Kathleen's foot, pushed against Bernard's waistcoat, sat down, partly on Mavis and partly on Francis and said — "Of all the impertinence!" Then someone banged the door — the train shivered and trembled and pulled itself together in the way we all know so well — grunted, snorted, screamed, and was off. Aunt Enid stood up arranging things on the rack, so that the children could not even see if the nice lady had found a seat in the train.

"Well — I do think — " Francis could not help saying.

"Oh — do you?" said Aunt Enid, "I should never have thought it of you."

When she had arranged the things in the rack to her satisfaction she pointed out a few little faults that she had noticed in the children and settled down to read a book by Miss Marie Corelli. The children looked miserably at each other. They could not understand why Mother had placed them under the control of this most unpleasant mock aunt.

There was a reason for it, of course. If your parents, who are generally so kind and jolly, suddenly do a thing that you can't understand and can hardly bear, you may be quite sure they have a good reason for it. The reason in this case was that Aunt Enid was the only person who offered to take charge of the children at a time when all the nice people who usually did it were having influenza. Also she was an old friend of Granny's. Granny's taste in friends must have been very odd, Francis decided, or else Aunt Enid must have changed a good deal since she was young. And there she sat reading her dull book. The children also had been provided with books — *Eric, or Little by Little; Elsie, or Like a Little Candle; Brave Bessie* and *Ingenious Isabel* had been dealt out as though they were cards for a game, before leaving home. They had been a great bother to carry, and they were impossible to read. Kathleen and Bernard presently preferred looking out of the windows, and the two elder ones tried to read the paper left by the lady, "looking over."

Now, that is just where it was, and really what all that has been written before is about. If that lady hadn't happened to look in at their door, and if she hadn't happened to leave the paper they would never have seen it, because they weren't the sort of children who read papers except under extreme provocation.

You will not find it easy to believe, and I myself can't see why it should have happened, but the very first word they saw in that newspaper was *Beachfield*, and the second was *On*, and the third was *Sea*, and the fifth was *Mermaid*. The fourth which came between *Sea* and *Mermaid* was *Alleged*.

"I say," said Mavis, "let's look."

"Don't pull then, you can see all right," said Francis, and this is what they read together:

BEACHFIELD-ON-SEA — ALLEGED MERMAID.
AMAZING STORY.

"At this season of the year, which has come to be designated the silly season, the public press is deluged with puerile old-world stories of gigantic gooseberries and enormous sea serpents. So that it is quite in keeping with the weird traditions of this time of the year to find a story of some wonder of the deep, arising even at so well-known a watering place as Beachfield. Close to an excellent golf course, and surrounded by various beauty spots, with a thoroughly revised water supply, a newly painted pier and three rival Cinematograph Picture Palaces, Beachfield has long been known as a rising plague of exceptional attractions, the quaint charm of its..."

"Hold on," said Francis, "this isn't about any old Mermaid."

"Oh, that'll be further on," said Mavis. "I expect they have to put all that stuff in to be polite to Beachfield — let's skip — *agreeable promenade, every modern convenience, while preserving its quaint...* What does *quaint* mean, and why do they keep on saying it?"

"I don't think it means anything," said Francis, "it's just a word they use, like weird and dainty. You always see it in a newspaper. Ah — got her. Here she is — *The excitement may be better imagined than described* — no, that's about the Gymkhana — here we are:

"Master Wilfred Wilson, the son of a well-known and respected resident, arrived home yesterday evening in tears. Inquiry elicited a statement that he had been paddling in the rock pools, which are to be found in such profusion under the West Cliff, when something gently pinched his foot. He feared that it might be a lobster, having read that these crustaceans sometimes attack the unwary intruder, and he screamed. So far his story, though

*unusual, contains nothing inherently impossible. But when he
went on to state that a noise "like a lady speaking" told him not
to cry, and that, on looking down, he perceived that what held
him was a hand "coming from one of the rocks under water," his
statement was naturally received with some incredulity. It was
not until a boating party returning from a pleasure trip
westward stated that they had seen a curious sort of white seal
with a dark tail darting through the clear water below their boat
that Master Wilfred's story obtained any measure of credence."*

("What's credence?" said Mavis.

"Oh, never mind. It's what you believe with, I think. Go on,"
said Francis.)

" *— of credence. Mr. Wilson, who seems to have urged an
early retirement to bed as a cure for telling stories and getting his
feet wet, allowed his son to rise and conduct him to the scene of
adventure. But Mr. Wilson, though he even went to the length of
paddling in some of the pools, did not see or feel any hands nor
hear any noise, ladylike or otherwise. No doubt the seal theory is
the correct one. A white seal would be a valuable acquisition to
the town, and would, no doubt, attract visitors. Several boats
have gone out, some with nets and some with lines. Mr.
Carrerras, a visitor from South America, has gone out with a
lariat, which in these latitudes is, of course, quite a novelty."*

"That's all," whispered Francis, and glanced at Aunt Enid. "I
say — she's asleep." He beckoned the others, and they screwed
themselves along to that end of the carriage farthest from the
slumbering aunt. "Just listen to this," he said. Then in hoarse
undertones he read all about the Mermaid.

"I say," said Bernard, "I do hope it's a seal. I've never seen a
seal."

"I hope they *do* catch it'" said Kathleen, "fancy seeing a real
live Mermaid."

"If it's a real live Mermaid I jolly well hope they don't catch her," said Francis.

"So do I," said Mavis. "I'm certain she would die in captivity."

"But I'll tell you what," said Francis, "we'll go and look for her, first thing tomorrow. I suppose," he added thoughtfully, "Sabrina was a sort of Mermaid."

"She hasn't a tail, you know," Kathleen reminded him.

"It isn't the tail that makes the Mermaid," Francis reminded her. "It's being able to live underwater. If it was the tail, then mackerels would be Mermaids."

"And, of course, they're not. I see," said Kathleen.

"I wish," said Bernard, "that she'd given us bows and arrows instead of pails and spades, and then we could have gone seal-shooting — "

"Or Mermaid-shooting," said Kathleen. "Yes, that would have been ripping."

Before Francis and Mavis could say how shocked they were at the idea of shooting Mermaids, Aunt Enid woke up and took the newspaper away from them, because newspapers are not fit reading for children.

She was somehow the kind of person before whom you never talk about anything that you really care for, and it was impossible therefore to pursue either seals or Mermaids. It seemed best to read *Eric* and the rest of the books. It was uphill work.

But the last two remarks of Bernard and Kathleen had sunk into the minds of the two elder children. That was why, when they had reached Beachfield and found Mother and rejoiced over her, and when Aunt Enid had unexpectedly gone on by that same train to stay with her really relations at Bournemouth, they did not say any more to the little ones about Mermaids or seals, but just joined freely in the chorus of pleasure at Aunt Enid's departure.

"I thought she was going to stay with us all the time," said Kathleen. "Oh, Mummy, I am so glad she isn't."

"Why? — don't you like Aunt Enid? Isn't she kind?"

All four thought of the spades and pails and shrimping nets, and of *Eric* and *Elsie* and the other books — and all said:

"Yes."

"Then what was it?" Mother asked. And they could not tell her. It is sometimes awfully difficult to tell things to your mother, however much you love her. The best Francis could do was:

"Well — you see we're not used to her."

And Kathleen said: "I don't think perhaps she's used to being an aunt. But she was kind."

And Mother was wise and didn't ask any more questions. Also she at once abandoned an idea one had had of asking Aunt Enid to come and stay at Beachfield for part of the holidays; and this was just as well, for if Aunt Enid had not passed out of the story exactly when she did, there would not have been any story to pass out of. And as she does now pass out of the story I will say that she thought she was very kind, and that she meant extremely well.

There was a little whispering between Francis and Mavis just after tea, and a little more just before bed, but it was tactfully done and the unwhispered-to younger ones never noticed it.

The lodgings were very nice — a little way out of the town — not a villa at all as everyone had feared. I suppose the landlady thought it grander to call it a villa, but it was really a house that had once been a mill house, and was all made of a soft-colored gray wood with a red-tiled roof, and at the back was the old mill, also gray and beautiful — not used now for what it was built for — but just as a store for fishing nets and wheel-barrows and old rabbit hutches and beehives and harness and odds and ends, and the sack of food for the landlady's chickens. There was a great corn bin there too — that must have been in some big stable — and some broken chairs and an old wooden cradle that hadn't had any babies in it since the landlady's mother was a little girl.

On any ordinary holiday the mill would have had all the charm of a magic palace for the children, with its wonderful collection of pleasant and unusual things to play with, but just now all their thoughts were on Mermaids. And the two elder ones decided that they would go out alone the first thing in the morning and look for the Mermaid.

Mavis woke Francis up very early indeed, and they got up and dressed quite quietly, not washing, I am sorry to say, because water makes such a noise when you pour it out. And I am afraid their hair was not very thoroughly brushed either. There was not a soul stirring in the road as they went out, unless you count the mill cat who had been out all night and was creeping home very tired and dusty looking, and a yellowhammer who sat on a tree a hundred yards down the road and repeated his name over and over again in that conceited way yellowhammers have, until they got close to him; and then he wagged his tail impudently at them and flew on to the next tree where he began to talk about himself as loudly as ever.

This desire to find the Mermaid must have been wonderfully strong in Francis, for it completely swallowed the longing of years — the longing to see the sea. It had been too dark the night before to see anything but the winking faces of the houses as the fly went past them. But now as he and Mavis ran noiselessly down the sandy path in their rubber shoes and turned the corner of the road, he saw a great pale-gray something spread out in front of him, lit with points of red and gold fire where the sun touched it. He stopped.

"Mavis," he said, in quite an odd voice, "that's the sea."

"Yes," she said and stopped too.

"It isn't a bit what I expected," he said, and went on running.

"Don't you like it?" asked Mavis, running after him.

"Oh — like," said Francis, "it isn't the sort of thing you *like*."

When they got down to the shore the sands and the pebbles were all wet because the tide had just gone down, and there were the rocks and the little rock pools, and the limpets, and whelks, and the little yellow periwinkles looking like particularly fine Indian corn all scattered among the red and the brown and the green seaweed.

"Now, this *is* jolly," said Francis. "This is jolly if you like. I almost wish we'd wakened the others. It doesn't seem quite fair."

"Oh, they've seen it before," Mavis said, quite truly, "and I don't think it's any good going by fours to look for Mermaids, do you?"

"Besides," said Francis, saying what had been in their thoughts since yesterday in the train, "Kathleen wanted to shoot Mermaids, and Bernard thought it was seals, anyhow."

They had sat down and were hastily pulling off their shoes and stockings.

"Of course," said he, "we shan't find anything. It isn't likely."

"Well," she said, "for anything we jolly well know, they may have found her already. Take care how you go over these rocks, they're awfully slippy."

"As if I didn't know that," said he, and ran across the narrow strip of sand that divided rocks from shingle and set his foot for the first time in The Sea. It was only a shallow little green and white rock pool, but it was the sea all the same.

"I say, isn't it cold," said Mavis, withdrawing pink and dripping toes; "do mind how you go — "

"As if I — " said Francis, again, and sat down suddenly and splashingly in a large, clear sparkling pool.

"Now, I suppose we've got to go home at once and you change," said Mavis, not without bitterness.

"Nonsense," said Francis, getting up with some difficulty and clinging wetly to Mavis to steady himself. "I'm quite dry, almost."

"You know what colds are like," said Mavis, "and staying indoors all day, or perhaps bed, and mustard plasters and gruel with butter in it. Oh, come along home, we should never have found the Mermaid. It's much too bright and light and everydayish for anything like magic to happen. Come on home, do."

"Let's just go out to the end of the rocks," Francis urged, "just to see what it's like where the water gets deep and the seaweed goes swish, swish, all long and lanky and grassy, like in the Sabrina picture."

"Halfway then, not more," said Mavis, firmly, "it's dangerous — deep outside — Mother said so."

And halfway they went, Mavis still cautious, and Francis, after his wetting, almost showing off in his fine carelessness of whether he went in again or not. It was very jolly. You know how soft and squeezy the blobby kind of seaweed is to walk on, and how satin smooth is the ribbon kind; how sharp are limpets, especially when they are covered with barnacles, and how comparatively bearable to the foot are the pale primrose-colored hemispheres of the periwinkle.

"Now," said Mavis, "come on back. We'll run all the way as soon as we get our shoes and stockings on for fear of colds."

"I almost wish we hadn't come," said Francis, turning with a face of gloom.

"You didn't really think we should find a Mermaid, did you?" Mavis asked, and laughed, though she was really annoyed with Francis for getting wet and cutting short this exciting morning game. But she was a good sister.

"It's all been so silly. Flopping into that pool, and talking and rotting, and just walking out and in again. We ought to have come by moonlight, and been very quiet and serious, and said —

"Sabrina fair
   Listen where thou art sitting"

"Ow — Hold on a minute. I've caught my foot in something."

Mavis stopped and took hold of her brother's arm to steady him; and as she did so both children plainly heard a voice that was not the voice of either of them. It was the sweetest voice in the world they thought, and it said:

"Save her. We die in captivity."

Francis looked down and had a sort of sudden sight of something white and brown and green that moved and went quickly down under the stone on which Mavis was standing. There was nothing now holding his foot.

"I say," he said, on a deep breath of awe and wonder, "did you hear that?"

"Of course, I heard it."

"We couldn't both have fancied it," he said, "I wish it had told us who to save, and where, and how — "

"Whose do you think that voice was?" Mavis asked softly.

"The Mermaid's," said Francis, "who else's could it have been?"

"Then the magic's really begun — "

"Mermaids aren't magic," he said, "anymore than flying fishes or giraffes are."

"But she came when you said *Sabrina fair*," said Mavis.

"Sabrina wasn't a Mermaid," said Francis firmly. "It's no use trying to join things on when they won't. Come on, we may as well be getting home."

"Mightn't she be?" suggested Mavis. "A Mermaid, I mean. Like salmon that live in rivers and go down to the sea."

"We Die in Captivity."

"I say, I never thought of that. How simply ripping if it turned out to be really Sabrina — wouldn't it be? But which do you suppose could be her — the one who spoke to us or the one she's afraid will die in captivity — the one she wants us to save."

They had reached the shore by now and Mavis looked up from turning her brown stockings right way out to say:

"I suppose we didn't really both fancy it. Could we have? Isn't there some sort of scientific magic that makes people think the same things as each other when it's not true at all, like with Indian mango tricks? Uncle Fred said so, you know, they call it *Tell-ee-something*."

"I'll tell *you* something," said Francis, urgent with shoelace, "if we keep on saying things weren't when we know perfectly well they were, we shall soon dish up any sort of chance of magic we may ever have had. When do you find people in books going on like that? They just say 'This is magic!' and behave as if it was. They don't go pretending they're not sure. Why, no magic would stand it."

"Aunt Dorothea once told me that all magic was like Prince Rupert's drop," Mavis owned: "if once you broke it there was nothing left but a little dust."

"That's just what I'm saying, isn't it? We've always felt there was magic right enough, haven't we? Well, now we've come across it, don't let's be silly and pretend. Let's believe in it as hard as ever we can. Mavis — shall we, eh? Believing in things makes them stronger. Aunt Dorothea said that too — you remember."

They stood up in their shoes.

"Shall we tell the others?" Mavis asked.

"We must," said Francis, "it would be so sneakish not to. But they won't believe us. We shall have to be like Cassandra and not mind."

"I only wish I knew who it is we've got to save," said Mavis.

Francis had a very strong and perfect feeling that they would know this all in good time. He could not have explained this, but he felt it. All he said was, "Let's run."

And they ran.

Kathleen and Bernard met them at the gate, dancing with excitement and impatience.

"Where have you been?" they cried and "What on earth?" and "Why, you're all wet, France."

"Down to the sea — shut up, I know I am — " their elder brother came in and passed up the path to the gate.

"You might have called us," said Kathleen in a more-in-sorrow-than-in-anger sort of voice, "but anyhow you've lost something by going out so early without us."

"Lost something. What?"

"Hearing the great news," said Bernard, and he added, "Aha!"

"What news?"

"Wouldn't you like to know?" Bernard was naturally annoyed at having been left out of the first expedition of the holidays. Anyone would have. Even you or I.

"Out with it," said Francis, with a hand on Bernard's ear. There came a yell from Bernard and Mother's voice from the window, saying, "Children, children."

"All right, Mummy. Now, Bear — don't be a young rotter. What's the news?"

"You're hurting my ear," was all Bernard's rejoinder.

"All right," said Francis, "we've got some news too. But we won't tell, will we, Mavis?"

"Oh *don't*," said Kathleen, "don't let's be sneaky, the very first day too. It's only that they've caught the Mermaid, and I'm afraid she'll die in captivity, like you said. What's yours?"

Francis had released Bernard's ear and now he turned to Mavis.

"So that's it," he said slowly — "who's got her?"

"The circus people. What's your news?" asked Kathleen eagerly.

"After brek," said Francis. "Yes, Mother, half a sec! I apologize about the ear, Bernard. We will tell you all. Oh, it's quite different from what you think. We meet and discuss the situation in the mill the minute we're free from brek. Agreed? Right! Yes, Mother, coming!"

"Then there must," Mavis whispered to Francis, "be *two* Mermaids. They can't both be Sabrina... then which...?"

"We've got to save one of them anyhow," Francis answered with the light of big adventure in his eye, *"they die in captivity."*

The Rescue

The great question, of course, was — Would Mother take them to the circus, or would she, if she wouldn't herself take them, let them go alone? She had once, in Buckinghamshire, allowed them to go to a traveling menagerie, after exacting from them a promise that they were not to touch any of the animals, and they had seen reason to regret their promise when the showman offered to let them stroke his tame performing wolf, who was so very like a collie. When they had said, "No, thank you," the showman had said, "Oh, frightened, are you? Run along home to Mammy then!" and the bystanders had laughed in a most insulting way. At a circus, of course, the horses and things aren't near enough for you to stroke them, so this time they might not be asked to promise. If Mother came with them her presence, though agreeable, would certainly add to the difficulties, already quite enough — as even Mavis could not but see — of rescuing the Mermaid. But suppose Mother didn't come with them.

"Suppose we have to promise we won't touch any of the animals?" suggested Cathay. "You can't rescue a person without touching it."

"That's just it," said Mavis, "a Mermaid isn't an animal. She's a person."

"But suppose it isn't that sort of Mermaid," said Bernard. "Suppose it's the sort that other people call seals, like it said in the paper."

"Well, it isn't," said Francis briefly, adding, "so there!"

They were talking in the front garden, leaning over the green gate while Mother upstairs unpacked the luggage that had been the mound with spades on top only yesterday, at Waterloo.

"Mavis!" Mother called through the open window. "I can only find — but you'd better come up.

"I ought to offer to help Mother unpack," said Mavis, and went walking slowly.

She came back after a little while, however, quickly running.

"It's all right," she said. "Mother's going to meet Daddy at the Junction this afternoon and buy us sunbonnets. And we're to take our spades and go down to the sea till dinnertime — it's roast rabbit and apple dumps — I asked Mrs. Pearce — and we can go to the circus by ourselves — and she never said a word about promise not to touch the animals."

So off they went, down the white road where the yellow-hammer was talking about himself as usual on the tree just beyond wherever you happened to be walking. And so to the beach.

Now it is very difficult to care much about a Mermaid you have never seen or heard or touched. On the other hand, when once you have seen one and touched one and heard one speak, you seem to care for very little else. This was why when they got to the shore Kathleen and Bernard began at once to dig the moat of a sand castle, while the elder ones walked up and down, dragging the new spades after them like some new kind of tail, and talking, talking, talking till Kathleen said they might help dig or the tide would be in before the castle was done.

"You don't know what a lark sand castles are, France," she added kindly, "because you've never seen the sea before."

So then they all dug and piled and patted and made molds of their pails to stand as towers to the castle and dug out dungeons and tunnels and bridges, only the roof always gave way in the end unless you had beaten the sand very tight beforehand. It was a glorious castle, though not quite finished when the first thin flat wash of the sea reached it. And then everyone worked twice as hard trying to keep the sea out till all was hopeless, and then everyone crowded into the castle and the sea washed it away bit by bit till there was only a shapeless island left, and everyone was wet through and had to change every single thing the minute they got home. You will know by that how much they enjoyed themselves.

After the roast rabbit and the apple dumplings Mother started on the sunbonnet-and-meet-Daddy expedition. Francis went with her to the station and returned a little sad.

"I had to promise not to touch any of the animals," he said. "And perhaps a Mermaid is an animal."

"Not if she can speak," said Kathleen. "I say, don't you think we ought to wear our best things — I do. It's more respectable to the wonders of the deep. She'd like us to look beautiful."

"I'm not going to change for anybody," said Bernard firmly.

"All right, Bear," said Mavis. "Only we will. Remember it's magic."

"I say, France," he said, "do you think we *ought* to change?"

"No, I don't," Francis answered. "I don't believe Mermaids care a bit what you've got on. You see, they don't wear anything but tails and hair and looking glasses themselves. If there's any beautifulness to be done they jolly well do it themselves. But I don't say you wouldn't be better for washing your hands again, and you might as well try to get *some* of the sand out of your hair. It looks like the wrong end of a broom as it is."

He himself went so far as to put on the blue necktie that Aunt Amy had given him, and polished his silver watch chain on the inside of his jacket. This helped to pass the time till the girls were ready. At last this happened though they had put on their best things, and they started.

The yellowhammer went on about himself — he was never tired of the subject.

"It's just as if that bird was making fun of us," Bernard said.

"I daresay it is a wild-goose step we're taking," said Kathleen; "but the circus will be jolly, anyhow."

There is a piece of wasteland just beyond Beachfield on the least agreeable side of that village — the side where the flat-faced shops are and the yellow brick houses. At the nice end of Beachfield the shops have little fat bow windows with greenish glass that you can hardly see through. Here also are gaunt hoardings plastered with tattered, ugly-colored posters, asking you in red to wear Ramsden's Really Boots or to Vote for Wilton Ashby in blue. Some of the corners of the posters are always loose and flap dismally in the wind. There is always a good deal of straw and torn paper and dust at this end of the village, and bits of dirty rag, and old boots and tins are found under the hedges where flowers ought to be. Also there are a great many nettles and barbed wires instead of pleasant-colored fences. Don't you sometimes wonder who is to blame for all the uglification of places that might be so pretty, and wish you could have a word with them and ask them not to? Perhaps when these people were little nobody told them how wrong it is to throw orange peel about, and the bits of paper off chocolate, and the paper bag which once concealed your bun. And it is a dreadful fact that the children who throw these things about are little uglifiers, and they grow up to be perfect monsters of uglification, and build hideous yellow brick cottages, and put up hoardings, and sell Ramsden's Really Boots (in red), and vote passionately for Wilton Ashby (in blue), and care nothing for the fields that used to be green and the hedges where once flowers used to grow. Some people like this, and see nothing to hate in such ugly waste places as the one, at the wrong end of the town, where the fair was being held on that never-to-be-forgotten day when Francis, Mavis, Bernard and Kathleen set out in their best clothes to rescue the Mermaid because Mermaids "die in captivity."

The fair had none of those stalls and booths which old-fashioned fairs used to have, where they sold toys, and gilt gingerbread, and carters' whips, and cups and saucers, and mutton pies, and dolls, and china dogs, and shell boxes, and pincushions, and needle cases, and penholders with views of the Isle of Wight and Winchester Cathedral inside that you see so bright and plain when you put your eye close to the little round hole at the top.

The steam roundabouts were there — but hardly a lean back of their spotted horses was covered by a rider. There were swings, but no one happened to be swinging. There were no shows, no menagerie, no boxing booth, no marionettes. No penny gaff with the spangled lady and the fat man who beats the drum. Nor were there any stalls. There were pink-and-white paper whips and bags of dust-colored minced paper — the English substitute for *confetti* — there were little metal tubes of dirty water to squirt in people's faces, but except for the sale of these crude instruments for making other people uncomfortable there was not a stall in the fair. I give you my word, there was not a single thing that you could buy — no gingerbread, no sweets, no crockery dogs, not even a half-penny orange or a bag of nuts. Nor was there anything to drink — not as much as a lemonade counter or a ginger beer stall. The revelers were no doubt drinking elsewhere. A tomblike silence reigned — a silence which all the steam roundabout's hideous hootings only emphasized.

A very dirty-nosed boy, overhearing a hurried council, volunteered the information that the circus had not yet opened.

"Never mind," they told each other — and turned to the side-shows. These were all of one character — the arrangement by which you throw something or roll something at something else, and if you hit the something you get a prize — the sort of prize that is sold in Houndsditch at nine pence a gross.

Most of these arrangements are so ordered that to get a prize is impossible. For instance, a peculiarly offensive row of masks with open mouths in which pipes are set up. In the golden days of long ago if you hit a pipe it broke — and you got a "prize" worth — I can't do sums — put it briefly at the hundred and forty-fourth part of nine pence. But the children found that when their wooden ball struck the pipe it didn't break. They wondered why! Then, looking more closely, they saw that the pipes were not of clay, but of painted wood. They could never be broken — and the whole thing was a cruel mockery of hope.

The coconut-shy was not what it used to be either. Once one threw sticks, three shies a penny. Now it is a penny a shy, with light wooden balls. You can win a coconut if you happen to hit one that is not glued onto its support. If you really wish to win one of these unkindly fruits it is well to stand and watch a little and not to aim at those coconuts which, when they are hit, fail to fall off the sticks. Are they glued on? One hopes not. But if they are, who can wonder or reprove? It is hard to get a living, anyhow.

There was one thing, though, that roused the children's resentment — chiefly, I think, because its owners were clean and did not look half-starved, so there was no barrier of pity between them and dislike — a sort of round table sloping up to its center. On this small objects were arranged. For a penny you received two hoops. If you could throw a hoop over an object that object was yours. None of the rustic visitors to the fair could, it seemed, or cared to. It did not look difficult, however. Nor was it. At the first shot a tiny candlestick was encircled. Between pride and shame Mavis held out a hand.

"Hard luck," said one of the two young women, too clean to be pitied. "Has to go flat on — see?"

Francis tried again. This time the ring encircled a matchbox, "flat on."

"Hard luck," said the lady again.

"What's the matter now?" the children asked, baffled.

"Hoop has to be red side up," said she. So she scored. Now they went to the other side and had another penn'orth of hoops from the other too clean young woman. And the same thing happened. Only on the second winning she said:

"Hard luck. Hoops have to be blue side up."

It was Bernard's blood that was up. He determined to clear the board.

"Blue side up, is it," he said sternly, and took another penn'orth. This time he brought down a tin pin tray and a little box which, I hope, contained something. The girl hesitated and then handed over the prizes. "Another penn'orth of hoops," said Bernard, warming to the work.

"Hard luck," said she. "We don't give more than two penn'orth to any one party."

The prizes were not the kind of things you care to keep, even as trophies of victory — especially when you have before you the business of rescuing a Mermaid. The children gave their prizes to a small female bystander and went to the shooting gallery. That, at least, could have no nonsense about it. If you aimed at a bottle and hit it it would break. No sordid self-seeking custodian could rob you of the pleasant tinkling of the broken bottle. And even with a poor weapon it is not impossible to aim at a bottle and hit it. This is true — but at the shooting gallery the trouble was *not* to hit the bottles. There were so many of them and they were so near. The children got thirteen tinkling smashes for their fourteen shots. The bottles were hung fifteen feet away instead of thirty. Why? Space is not valuable at the fair — can it be that the people of Sussex are such poor shots that thirty feet is to them a prohibitive distance?

They did not throw for coconuts, nor did they ride on the little horses or pull themselves to dizzy heights in the swings. There was no heart left in them for such adventures — and besides everyone in the fair, saving themselves and the small female bystander and the hoop girls, was dirtier than you would believe possible. I suppose Beachfield has a water supply. But you would have doubted it if you had been at the fair. They heard no laughter, no gay talk, no hearty give-and-take of holiday jests. A dull heavy silence brooded over the place, and you could hear that silence under the shallow insincere gaiety of the steam roundabout.

Laughter and song, music and good-fellowship, dancing and innocent revelry, there were none of these at Beachfield Fair. For music there was the steam roundabout's echoes of the sordid musical comedy of the year before the year before last — laughter there was not — nor revelry — only the dirty guardians of the machines for getting your pennies stood gloomily huddled, and a few groups of dejected girls and little boys shivered in the cold wind that had come up with the sunset. In that wind too, danced the dust, the straw, the newspaper and the chocolate wrappers. The only dancing there was. The big tent that held the circus was at the top of the ground, and the people who were busy among the ropes and pegs and between the bright vans resting on their shafts seemed gaier and cleaner than the people who kept the little arrangements for people not to win prizes at. And now the circus at last was opened; the flap of the tent was pinned back, and a gypsy-looking woman, with oily black ringlets and eyes like bright black beads, came out at the side to take the money of those who wished to see the circus. People were now strolling toward it in twos and threes, and of these our four were the very first, and the gypsy woman took four warm six pences from their four hands.

"Walk in, walk in, my little dears, and see the white elephant," said a stout, black-mustached man in evening dress — greenish it was and shiny about the seams. He flourished a long whip as he spoke, and the children stopped, although they had paid their sixpences, to hear what they were to see when they did walk in. "The white elephant — tail, trunk, and tusks all complete, six pence only. See the Back Try A or Camels, or Ships of the Arabs — heavy drinker when he gets the chance — total abstainer while crossing the desert. Walk up, walk up. See the Trained Wolves and Wolverines in their great National Dance with the flags of all countries. Walk up, walk up, walk up. See the Educated Seals and the Unique Lotus of the Heast in her famous bare-backed act, riding three horses at once, the wonder and envy of royalty. Walk up and see the very table Mermaid caught on your own coast only yesterday as ever was."

"Thank you," said Francis, "I think we will." And the four went through the opened canvas into the pleasant yellow dusty twilight which was the inside of a squarish sort of tent, with an opening at the end, and through that opening you could see the sawdust-covered ring of the circus and benches all round it, and two men just finishing covering the front benches with red cotton strips.

"Where's the Mermaid?" Mavis asked a little boy in tights and a spangled cap.

"In there," he said, pointing to a little canvas door at the side of the squarish tent. "I don't advise you to touch her, though. Spiteful, she is. Lashes out with her tail — splashed old Mother Lee all over water she did — an' dangerous too: our Bill 'e got 'is bone set out in his wrist a-trying to hold on to her. An' it's thruppence extry to see her close."

There are times, as we all know, when three pence extra is a baffling obstacle — a cruel barrier to desire, but this was not, fortunately, such a moment. The children had plenty of money, because Mother had given them two half-crowns between them to spend as they liked.

"Even then," said Bernard, in allusion to the three pence extra, "we shall have two bob left."

So Mavis, who was treasurer, paid over the extra threepences to a girl with hair as fair and lank as hemp, and a face as brown and round as a tea cake, who sat on a kitchen chair by the Mermaid door. Then one by one they went in through the narrow opening, and at last there they were alone in the little canvas room with a tank in it that held — well, there was a large label, evidently written in a hurry, for the letters were badly made and arranged quite crookedly, and this label declared:

REAL LIVE MERMAID.
SAID TO BE FABULUS, BUT NOW TRUE.
CAUGHT HERE.
PLEASE DO NOT TOUCH.
DANGEROUS.

The little Spangled Boy had followed them in and pointed to the last word.

"What I tell you?" he asked proudly.

The children looked at each other. Nothing could be done with this witness at hand. At least...

"Perhaps if it's going to be magic," Mavis whispered to Francis, "outsiders wouldn't notice. They don't sometimes — I believe. Suppose you just said a bit of 'Sabrina' to start the magic."

"Wouldn't be safe," Francis returned in the same low tones. "Suppose he *wasn't* an outsider, and *did* notice."

So there they stood helpless. What the label was hung on was a large zinc tank — the kind that they have at the tops of houses for the water supply — you must have seen one yourself often when the pipes burst in frosty weather, and your father goes up into the roof of the house with a candle and pail, and the water drips through the ceilings and the plumber is sent for, and comes when it suits him. The tank was full of water and at the bottom of it could be seen a mass of something dark that looked as if it were partly browny-green fish and partly greeny-brown seaweed.

"Sabrina fair," Francis suddenly whispered, "send him away."

And immediately a voice from outside called "Rube — Reuben — drat the boy, where's he got to?" — and the little spangled intruder had to go.

"There, now," said Mavis, "if *that* isn't magic!" Perhaps it was, but still the dark fish-and-seaweed heap in the tank had not stirred. "Say it all through," said Mavis.

"Yes, do," said Bernard, "then we shall know for certain whether it's a seal or not."

So once again —

"Sabrina fair,
    Listen where thou art sitting,
    Under the glassie, cool, translucent wave,"

He got no further. There was a heaving and stirring of the seaweed and fish tail, something gleamed white, through the brown something white parted the seaweed, two white hands parted it, and a face came to the surface of the rather dirty water and — there was no doubt about it — spoke.

"*Translucent wave*, indeed!" was what the face said. "I wonder you're not ashamed to speak the invocation over a miserable cistern like this. What do you want?"

Brown hair and seaweed still veiled most of the face, but all the children, who, after their first start back had pressed close

"Translucent Wave, Indeed!"

to the tank again, could see that the face looked exceedingly cross.

"We want," said Francis in a voice that would tremble though he told himself again and again that he was not a baby and wasn't going to behave like one — "we want to help you."

"Help *me*? You?" She raised herself a little more in the tank and looked contemptuously at them. "Why, don't you know that I am mistress of all water magic? I can raise a storm that will sweep away this horrible place and my detestable captors and you with them, and carry me on the back of a great wave down to the depths of the sea."

"Then why on earth don't you?" Bernard asked.

"Well, I was thinking about it," she said, a little awkwardly, "when you interrupted with your spells. Well, you've called and I've answered — now tell me what I can do for you."

"We've told you," said Mavis gently enough, though she was frightfully disappointed that the Mermaid after having in the handsomest manner turned out to *be* a Mermaid, should be such a very short-tempered one. And when they had talked about her all day and paid the threepence each extra to see her close, and put on their best white dresses too. "We've told you — we want to help you. Another Sabrina in the sea told us to. *She* didn't tell us anything about you being a magic-mistress. She just said 'they die in captivity.' "

"Well, thank you for coming," said the Mermaid. "If she really said that it must be one of two things — either the sun is in the House of Liber — which is impossible at this time of the year — or else the rope I was caught with must be made of llama's hair, and *that's* impossible in these latitudes. Do you know anything about the rope they caught me with?"

"No," said Bernard and Kathleen. But the others said, "it was a lariat."

"Ah," said the Mermaid, "my worst fears are confirmed — But who could have expected a lariat on these shores? But that must have been it. Now I know why, though I have been on the point of working the magic of the Great Storm at least five hundred times since my capture, some unseen influence has always held me back."

"You mean," said Bernard, "you feel that it wouldn't work, so you didn't try."

A rattling, ripping sound outside, beginning softly, waxed louder and louder so as almost to drown their voices. It was the drum, and it announced the beginning of the circus. The Spangled Child put his head in and said, "Hurry up or you'll miss my Infant Prodigious Act on the Horse with the Tambourines," and took his head out again.

"Oh, dear," said Mavis, "and we haven't arranged a single thing about rescuing you."

"No more you have," said the Mermaid carelessly.

"Look here," said Francis, "you do *want* to be rescued, don't you?"

"Of course I do," replied the Mermaid impatiently, "now I know about the llama rope. But I can't walk even if they'd let me, and you couldn't carry me. Couldn't you come at dead of night with a chariot — I could lift myself into it with your aid — then you could drive swiftly hence, and driving into the sea I could drop from the chariot and escape while you swam ashore."

"I don't believe we could — any of it," said Bernard, "let alone swimming ashore with horses and chariots. Why, Pharaoh himself couldn't do that, you know." And even Mavis and Francis added helplessly, "I don't see how we're to get a chariot," and "do you think of some other way."

"I shall await you," said the lady in the tank with perfect calmness, "at dead of night."

With that she twisted the seaweed closely around her head and shoulders and sank slowly to the bottom of the tank. And the children were left staring blankly at each other, while in the circus tent music sounded and the soft heavy pad-pad of hoofs on sawdust.

"What shall we do?" Francis broke the silence.

"Go and see the circus, of course," said Bernard.

"Of course, we can talk about the chariot afterwards," Mavis admitted.

"There'll be lots of time to talk between now and dead of night," said Kathleen. "Come on, Bear."

And they went.

There is nothing like a circus for making you forget your anxieties. It is impossible to dwell on your troubles and difficulties when performing dogs are displaying their accomplishments, and wolves dancing their celebrated dance with the flags of all nations, and the engaging lady who jumps through the paper hoops and comes down miraculously on the flat back of the white horse, cannot but drive dull care away, especially from the minds of the young. So that for an hour and a half — it really was a good circus, and I can't think how it happened to be at Beachfield Fair at all — a solid slab of breathless enjoyment was wedged in between the interview with the Mermaid and the difficult task of procuring for her the chariot she wanted. But when it was all over and they were part of a hot, tightly packed crowd pouring out of the dusty tent into the sunshine, their responsibilities came upon them with renewed force.

"Wasn't the clown ripping?" said Bernard, as they got free of the crowd.

"I liked the riding-habit lady best, and the horse that went like that, best," said Kathleen, trying with small pale hands and brown shod legs to give an example of a horse's conduct during an exhibition of the *haute école*.

"Didn't you think the elephant — " Mavis was beginning, when Francis interrupted her.

"About that chariot," he said, and after that they talked of nothing else. And whatever they said it always came to this in the end, that they hadn't got a chariot, and couldn't get a chariot, and that anyhow they didn't suppose there was a chariot to *be* got, at any rate in Beachfield.

"It wouldn't be any good, I suppose," said Kathleen's last and most helpful suggestion — "be the slightest good saying 'Sabrina fair' to a pumpkin?"

"We haven't got even a pumpkin," Bernard reminded her, "let alone the rats and mice and lizards that Cinderella had. No, that's no good. But I'll tell you what." He stopped short. They were near home now — it was late afternoon, in the road where the talkative yellowhammer lived. "What about a wheelbarrow?"

"Not big enough," said Francis.

"There's an extra big one in the mill," said Bernard. "Now, look here. I'm not any good at magic. But Uncle Tom said I was a born general. If I tell you exactly what to do, will you two do it, and let Cathay and me off going?"

"Going to sneak out of it?" Francis asked bitterly.

"It isn't. It's not my game at all, and I don't want to play. And if I do, the whole thing will be muffed — you know it will. I'm so unlucky. You'd never get out at dead of night without me dropping a boot on the stairs or sneezing — you know you wouldn't."

Bernard took a sort of melancholy pride in being the kind of boy who always gets caught. If you are that sort of boy, perhaps that's the best way to take it. And Francis could not deny that there was something in what he said. He went on: "Then Kathleen's my special sister and I'm not going to have her dragged into a row. ("I want to," Kathleen put in ungratefully.) So will you and Mavis do it on your own or not?"

After some discussion, in which Kathleen was tactfully dealt with, it was agreed that they would. Then Bernard unfolded his plan of campaign.

"Directly we get home," he said, "we'll begin larking about with that old wheelbarrow — giving each other rides, and so on, and when it's time to go in we'll leave it at the far end of the field behind the old sheep hut near the gate. Then it'll be handy for you at dead of night. You must take towels or something and tie around the wheel so that it doesn't make a row. You can sleep with my toy alarm under your pillow and it won't wake anyone but you. You get out through the dining room window and in the same way. I'll lend you my new knife, with three blades and a corkscrew, if you'll take care of it, to cut the canvas, and go by the back lane that comes out behind where the circus is, but if you took my advice you wouldn't go at all. She's not a nice Mermaid at all. I'd rather have had a seal, any day. Hullo, there's Daddy and Mother. Come on."

They came on.

The program sketched by Bernard was carried out without a hitch. Everything went well, only Francis and Mavis were both astonished to find themselves much more frightened than they had expected to be. Any really great adventure like the rescuing of a Mermaid does always look so very much more serious when you carry it out, at night, than it did when you were planning it in the daytime. Also, though they knew they were not doing anything wrong, they had an uncomfortable feeling that Mother and Daddy might not agree with them on that point. And, of course, they could not ask leave to go and rescue a Mermaid, with a chariot, at dead of night. It is not the sort of thing you *can* ask leave to do, somehow. And the more you explained your reasons the less grown-up people would think you fitted to conduct such an expedition.

Francis lay down fully dressed, under his nightshirt. And Mavis under hers wore her short blue skirt and jersey. The alarm, true to its trust, went off into an ear-splitting whizz and bang under the pillow of Francis, but no one else heard it. He crept cautiously into Mavis's room and wakened her, and as they crept down in stockinged feet not a board creaked. The French window opened without noise, the wheelbarrow was where they had left it, and they had fortunately brought quite enough string to bind wads of towels and stockings to the tire of its wheel. Also they had not forgotten the knife.

The wheelbarrow was heavy and they rather shrank from imagining how much heavier it would be when the discontented Mermaid was curled up in it. However, they took it in turns, and got along all right by the back lane that comes out above the waste ground where Beachfield holds its fairs.

"I hope the night's dead enough," Mavis whispered as the circus came in sight, looking very white in the starlight, "it's nearly two by now I should think."

"Quite dead enough, if that's all," said Francis; "but suppose the gypsies are awake? They do sit up to study astronomy to tell fortunes with, don't they? Suppose this is their astronomy night? I vote we leave the barrow here and go and reconnoiter."

They did. Their sandshoes made no noise on the dewy grass, and treading very carefully, on tiptoe, they came to the tent. Francis nearly tumbled over a guy rope; he just saw it in time to avoid it.

"If I'd been Bernard I should have come a beastly noisy cropper over that," he told himself. They crept around the tent till they came to the little square bulge that marked the place where the tank was and the seaweed and the Mermaid.

"They die in captivity, they die in captivity, they die in captivity," Mavis kept repeating to herself, trying to keep up her courage by reminding herself of the desperately urgent nature of the adventure. "It's a matter of life and death," she told herself — "life and death."

And now they picked their way between the pegs and guy ropes and came quite close to the canvas. Doubts of the strength and silence of the knife possessed the trembling soul of Francis. Mavis's heart was beating so thickly that, as she said afterward, she could hardly hear herself think. She scratched gently on the canvas, while Francis felt for the knife with the three blades and the corkscrew. An answering signal from the imprisoned Mermaid would, she felt, give her fresh confidence. There was no answering scratch. Instead, a dark line appeared to run up the canvas — it was an opening made by the two hands of the Mermaid which held back the two halves of the tent side, cut neatly from top to bottom. Her white face peered out.

"Where is the chariot?" she asked in the softest of whispers, but not too soft to carry to the children the feeling that she was, if possible, crosser than ever.

Francis was afraid to answer. He knew that his voice could never be subdued to anything as soft as the voice that questioned him, a voice like the sound of tiny waves on a summer night, like the whisper of wheat when the wind passes through it on a summer morning. But he pointed toward the lane where they had left the wheelbarrow and he and Mavis crept away to fetch it.

As they wheeled it down the waste place both felt how much they owed to Bernard. But for his idea of muffling the wheel they could never have got the clumsy great thing down that bumpy uneven slope. But as it was they and the barrow stole towards the gypsy's tent as silently as the Arabs in the poem stole away with theirs, and they wheeled it close to the riven tent side. Then Mavis scratched again, and again the tent opened.

"Have you any cords?" the soft voice whispered, and Francis pulled what was left of the string from his pocket.

She had made two holes in the tent side, and now passing the string through these she tied back the flaps of the tent.

"Now," she said, raising herself in the tank and resting her hands on its side. "You must both help — take hold of my tail and lift. Creep in — one on each side."

It was a wet, sloppy, slippery, heavy business, and Mavis thought her arms would break, but she kept saying: "Die in captivity," and just as she was feeling that she could not bear it another minute the strain slackened and there was the Mermaid curled up in the barrow.

"Now," said the soft voice, "go — quickly."

It was all very well to say go quickly. It was as much as the two children could do, with that barrow-load of dripping Mermaid, to go at all. And very, very slowly they crept up the waste space. In the lane, under cover of the tall hedges, they paused.

"Go on," said the Mermaid.

"We can't till we've rested a bit" said Mavis panting. "How did you manage to get that canvas cut?"

"My shell knife, of course," said the person in the wheelbarrow. "We always carry one in our hair, in case of sharks."

"I see," said Francis, breathing heavily. "You had much better go on," said the barrow's occupant. "This chariot is excessively uncomfortable and much too small. Besides, delays are dangerous."

"We'll go in half a sec," said Francis, and Mavis added kindly: "You're really quite safe now, you know."

"*You* aren't," said the Mermaid. "I don't know whether you realize that I'm stolen property and that it will be extremely awkward for you if you are caught with me."

"But we shan't be caught with you," said Mavis hopefully.

"Everybody's sound asleep," said Francis. It was wonderful how brave and confident they felt now that the deed was done. "It's perfectly safe. — Oh, what's that! Oh!"

A hand had shot from the black shadow of the hedge and caught him by the arm.

"What is it, France? What is it?" said Mavis, who could not see what was happening.

"What is it — now what is it?" asked the Mermaid more crossly than she had yet spoken.

"*Who* is it? Oh, who is it?" gasped Francis, writhing in the grip of his invisible assailant. And from the dark shadow of the hedge came the simple and terrible reply:

"The police!"

Gratitude

It is hardly possible to imagine a situation less attractive than that of Mavis and Francis — even the position of the Mermaid curled up in a dry barrow and far from her native element was not exactly luxurious. Still, she was no worse off than she had been when the lariat first curled itself about her fishy extremity. But the children! They had braved the terrors of night in an adventure of singular courage and daring, they had carried out their desperate enterprise, the Mermaid was rescued, and success seemed near — no further off than the sea indeed, and that, in point of fact, was about a quarter of a mile away. To be within a quarter of a mile of achievement, and then to have the cup of victory dashed from your lips, the crown of victory torn from your brow by — the police!

It was indeed hard. And what was more, it was dangerous.

"We shall pass the night in the cells," thought Mavis, in agony; "and whatever will Mother do when she finds we're gone?" In her mind "the cells" were underground dungeons, dark and damp and vaulted, where toads and lizards crawled, and no daylight ever penetrated. That is how dungeons are described in books about the Inquisition.

When the voice from the bush had said "The police," a stricken silence followed. The mouth of Francis felt dry inside, just as if he had been eating cracknels, he explained afterwards, and he had to swallow nothing before he could say:

"What for?"

"Let go his arm," said Mavis to the hidden foe. "We won't run away. Really we won't."

"You can't," said the Mermaid. "You can't leave me."

"Leave go," said Francis, wriggling. And then suddenly Mavis made a dart at the clutching hand and caught it by the wrist and whispered savagely:

"It's not a policeman at all. Come out of that bush — come out," and dragged. And something did come out of the bush. Something that certainly was not a policeman. It was small and thin, whereas policemen are almost always tall and stout. It did not wear the blue coats our Roberts wear, but velveteen knickerbockers and a tweed jacket. It was, in fact, a very small boy.

Francis broke into a cackle of relief.

"You little — animal," he said. "What a fright you gave me."

"Animal yourself, if you come to that, let alone her and her tail," the boy answered; and Mavis thought his voice didn't sound unfriendly. "My! But I did take a rise out of you that time, eh? Ain't she bit you yet, nor yet strook you with that there mackerel-end of hers?"

And then they recognized him. It was the little Spangled Boy. Only now, of course, being off duty he was no more spangled than you and I are.

"Whatever did you do it for?" Mavis asked crossly. "It was horrid of you."

"It wasn't only just a lark," said the boy. "I cut around and listened this afternoon when you was jawing, and I thought why not be in it? Only I do sleep that heavy, what with the riding and the tumbling and all. So I didn't wake till you'd got her out

THE POLICE.

and then I cut up along ahind the hedge to be beforehand with you. An' I was. It was a fair cop, matey, eh?"

"What are you going to do about it?" Francis asked flatly; "tell your father?" But Mavis reflected that he didn't seem to have told his father yet, and perhaps wouldn't.

"Ain't got no father," said the Spangled Boy, "nor yet mother."

"If you are rested enough you'd better go on," said the Mermaid. "I'm getting dry through."

And Mavis understood that to her that was as bad as getting wet through would be to us.

"I'm so sorry," she said gently, "but — "

"I must say I think it's very inconsiderate of you to keep me all this time in the dry," the Mermaid went on. "I really should have thought that even *you* — "

But Francis interrupted her.

"What are you going to *do*?" he asked the Spangled Boy. And that surprising child answered, spitting on his hands and rubbing them:

"Do? Why, give a 'and with the barrer."

The Mermaid put out a white arm and touched him.

"You are a hero," she said. "I can recognize true nobility even under a once-spangled exterior. You may kiss my hand."

"Well, of all the..." said Francis.

"Shall I?" the boy asked, more of himself than of the others.

"Do," Mavis whispered. "Anything to keep her in a good temper."

So the Spangled Boy kissed the still dampish hand of the Lady from the Sea, took the handles of the barrow and off they all went.

Mavis and Francis were too thankful for this unexpected help to ask any questions, though they could not help wondering exactly what it felt like to be a boy who did not mind stealing his own father's Mermaid. It was the boy himself who offered, at the next rest-halt, an explanation.

"You see," he said, "it's like this here. This party in the barrow — "

"I know you don't mean it disrespectfully," said the Mermaid, sweetly; "but *not* party — and *not* a barrow."

"Lady," suggested Mavis

"This lydy in the chariot, she'd been kidnapped — that's how I look at it. Same as what I was."

This was romance indeed; and Mavis recognized it and said: "You kidnapped? I say!"

"Yus," said Spangles, "when I was a baby kid. Old Mother Romaine told me, just afore she was took all down one side and never spoke no more."

"But why?" Mavis asked. "I never could understand in the books why gypsies kidnapped babies. They always seem to have so many of their own — far, far more than anyone could possibly want."

"Yes, indeed," said the Mermaid, "they prodded at me with sticks — a multitude of them."

"It wasn't kids as was wanted," said the boy, "it was revenge. That's what Mother Romaine said — my father he was a sort of Beak, so he give George Lee eighteen months for poaching. An' the day they took him the church bells was ringing like mad, and George, as he was being took, he said: *What's all that row? It ain't Sunday.* And then they tells him as how the bells was ringing 'cause him that was the Beak — my father, you know, — he'd got a son and hare. And that was me. You wouldn't think it to look at me," he added, spitting pensively and taking up the barrow handles, "but I'm a son and hare."

"And then what happened?" Mavis asked as they trudged on.

"Oh, George — he done his time, and I was a kiddy then, year-and-a-half old, all lace and ribbons and blue shoes made of glove-stuff, and George pinched me, and it makes me breff short, wheeling and talking."

"Pause and rest, my spangled friend," said the Mermaid in a voice of honey, "and continue your thrilling narrative."

"There ain't no more to it," said the boy, "except that I got one of the shoes. Old Mother Romaine 'ad kep' it, and a little shirt like a lady's handkercher, with R. V. on it in needlework. She didn't ever tell me what part of the country my dad was Beak in. Said she'd tell me next day. An' then there wasn't no next day for her — not fer telling things in, there wasn't."

He rubbed his sleeve across his eyes.

"She wasn't half a bad sort," he explained.

"Don't cry," said Mavis unwisely.

"Cry? Me?" he answered scornfully. "I've got a cold in me 'ead. You oughter know the difference between a cold in the head and sniveling. You been to school, I lay? — they might have taught you that."

"I wonder the gypsies didn't take the shoe and the shirt away from you?"

"Nobody know'd I'd got 'em; I always kep' em inside my shirt, wrapt up in a bit of paper, and when I put on me tights I used to hide 'em. I'm a-going to take the road one of these days, and find out who it was lost a kid with blue shoes and shirt nine years come April."

"Then you're ten and a half," said Mavis.

And the boy answered admiringly:

"How do you do it in your head so quick, miss? Yes, that's what I am."

Here the wheelbarrow resumed its rather bumpety progress, and nothing more could be said till the next stoppage, which was at that spot where the sea-front road swings around and down, and glides into the beach so gently that you can hardly tell where one begins and the other ends. It was much lighter there than up on the waste space. The moon was just breaking through a fluffy white cloud and cast a trembling sort of reflection on the sea. As they came down the slope all hands were needed to steady the barrow, because as soon as she saw the sea the Mermaid began to jump up and down like a small child at a Christmas tree.

"Oh, look!" she cried, "isn't it beautiful? Isn't it the only home in the world?"

"Not quite," said the boy.

"Ah!" said the lady in the barrow, "of course you're heir to one of the — what is it..."

"*Stately homes of England — how beautiful they stand*," said Mavis.

"Yes," said the lady. "I knew by instinct that he was of noble birth."

> "I bid ye take care of the brat," said he,
> "For he comes of a noble race,"

Francis hummed. He was feeling a little cross and sore. He and Mavis had had all the anxious trouble of the adventure, and now the Spangled Boy was the only one the Mermaid was nice to. It was certainly hard.

"But your stately home would not do for me at all," she went on. "My idea of home is all seaweed of coral and pearl — so cosy and delightful and wet. Now — can you push the chariot to the water's edge, or will you carry me?"

"Not much we won't," the Spangled Boy answered firmly. "We'll push you as far as we can, and then you'll have to wriggle."

"I will do whatever you suggest," she said amiably; "but what is this wriggle of which you speak?"

"Like a worm," said Francis.

"Or an eel," said Mavis.

"Nasty low things," said the Mermaid; and the children never knew whether she meant the worm and the eel, or the girl and the boy.

"Now then. All together," said the Spangled Child. And the barrow bumped down to the very edge of the rocks. And at the very edge its wheel caught in a chink and the barrow went sideways. Nobody could help it, but the Mermaid was tumbled out of her chariot on to the seaweed.

The seaweed was full and cushiony and soft, and she was not hurt at all — but she was very angry.

"You have been to school," she said, "as my noble preserver reminds you. You might have learned how not to upset chariots."

"It's we who are your preservers," Francis couldn't help saying.

"Of course you are," she said coolly, "plain preservers. Not noble ones. But I forgive you. You can't help being common and clumsy. I suppose it's your nature — just as it's his to be..."

"Good-bye," said Francis, firmly.

"Not at all," said the lady. "You must come with me in case there are any places where I can't exercise the elegant and vermiform accomplishment you spoke about. Now, one on each side, and one behind, and don't walk on my tail. You can't think how annoying it is to have your tail walked on."

"Oh, can't I," said Mavis. "I'll tell you something. My mother has a tail too."

"I *say!*" said Francis.

But the Spangled Child understood.

"She don't wear it every day, though," he said; and Mavis is almost sure that he winked. Only it is so difficult to be sure about winks in the starlight.

"Your mother must be better born than I supposed," said the Mermaid. "Are you *quite* sure about the tail?"

"I've trodden on it often," said Mavis — and then Francis saw.

Wriggling and sliding and pushing herself along by her hands, and helped now and then by the hands of the others, the Mermaid was at last got to the edge of the water.

"How glorious! In a moment I shall be quite wet," she cried.

In a moment everyone else was quite wet also — for with a movement that was something between a squirm and a jump, she dropped from the edge with a splashing flop.

And disappeared entirely.

AND DISAPPEARED ENTIRELY.

Consequences

The three children looked at each other.

"Well!" said Mavis.

"I do think she's ungrateful," said Francis.

"What did you expect?" asked the Spangled Child.

They were all wet through. It was very late — they were very tired, and the clouds were putting the moon to bed in a very great hurry. The Mermaid was gone; the whole adventure was ended.

There was nothing to do but to go home, and go to sleep, knowing that when they woke the next morning it would be to a day in the course of which they would have to explain their wet clothes to their parents.

"Even *you'll* have to do that," Mavis reminded the Spangled Boy.

He received her remark in what they afterward remembered to have been a curiously deep silence.

"I don't know how on earth we *are* to explain," said Francis. "I really don't. Come on — let's get home. No more adventures for me, thank you. Bernard knew what he was talking about."

Mavis, very tired indeed, agreed.

They had got over the beach by this time, recovered the

wheelbarrow, and trundled it up and along the road. At the corner the Spangled Boy suddenly said:

"Well then, so long, old sports," and vanished down a side lane.

The other two went on together — with the wheelbarrow, which, I may remind you, was as wet as any of them.

They went along by the hedge and the mill and up to the house.

Suddenly Mavis clutched at her brother's arm.

"There's a light," she said, "in the house."

There certainly was, and the children experienced that terrible empty sensation only too well known to all of us — the feeling of the utterly-found-out.

They could not be sure which window it was, but it was a downstairs window, partly screened by ivy. A faint hope still buoyed up Francis of getting up to bed unnoticed by whoever it was that had the light; and he and his sister crept around to the window out of which they had crept; but such a very long time ago it seemed. The window was shut.

Francis suggested hiding in the mill and trying to creep in unobserved later on, but Mavis said:

"No. I'm too tired for anything. I'm too tired to *live*, I think. Let's go and get it over, and then we can go to bed and sleep, and sleep, and sleep."

So they went and peeped in at the kitchen window, and there was no one but Mrs. Pearce, and she had a fire lighted and was putting a big pot on it.

The children went to the backdoor and opened it.

"You're early, for sure," said Mrs. Pearce, not turning.

This seemed a bitter sarcasm. It was too much. Mavis answered it with a sob. And at that Mrs. Pearce turned very quickly.

"What to gracious!" she said — "whatever to gracious is the matter? Where've you been?" She took Mavis by the shoulder. "Why, you're all sopping wet. You naughty, naughty little gell, you. Wait till I tell your Ma — been shrimping I lay — or trying to — never asking when the tide was right. And not a shrimp to show for it, I know, with the tide where it is. You wait till we hear what your Ma's got to say about it. And look at my clean flags and you dripping all over 'em like a fortnight's wash in wet weather."

Mavis twisted a little in Mrs. Pearce's grasp. "Oh, don't scold us, dear Mrs. Pearce," she said, putting a wet arm up toward Mrs. Pearce's neck. "We *are* so miserable."

"And so you deserve to be," said Mrs. Pearce, smartly. "Here, young chap, you go into the washhouse and get them things off, and drop them outside the door, and have a good rub with the jack-towel; and little miss can undress by the fire and put hem in this clean pail — and I'll pop up softlike and so as your Ma don't hear, and bring you down something dry.

A gleam of hope fell across the children's hearts — a gleam wild and watery as that which the moonlight had cast across the sea, into which the Mermaid had disappeared. Perhaps after all Mrs. Pearce wasn't going to tell Mother. If she was, why should she pop up softlike? Perhaps she would keep their secret. Perhaps she would dry their clothes. Perhaps, after all, that impossible explanation would never have to be given.

The kitchen was a pleasant place, with bright brasses and shining crockery, and a round three-legged table with a clean cloth and blue-and-white teacups on it.

Mrs. Pearce came down with their nightgowns and the warm dressing gowns that Aunt Enid had put in in spite of their expressed wishes. How glad they were of them now!

"There, that's a bit more like," said Mrs. Pearce; "here, don't look as if I was going to eat you, you little Peter Grievouses. I'll hot up some milk and here's a morsel of bread and dripping to keep the cold out. Lucky for you I was up — getting the boys' breakfast ready. The boats'll be in directly. The boys will laugh when I tell them — laugh fit to bust their selves they will."

"Oh, don't tell," said Mavis, "don't, please don't. Please, please don't."

"Well, I like that," said Mrs. Pearce, pouring herself some tea from a pot which, the children learned later, stood on the hob all day and most of the night; "it's the funniest piece I've heard this many a day. Shrimping at high tide!"

"I thought," said Mavis, "perhaps you'd forgive us, and dry our clothes, and not tell anybody."

"Oh, you did, did you?" said Mrs. Pearce. "Anything else—?"

"No, nothing else, thank you," said Mavis, "only I want to say thank you for being so kind, and it isn't high tide yet, and please we haven't done any harm to the barrow — but I'm afraid it's rather wet, and we oughtn't to have taken it without asking, I know, but you were in bed and — "

"The barrow?" Mrs. Pearce repeated, — "that great hulking barrow — you took the barrow to bring the shrimps home in? No — I can't keep it to myself — that really I can't — " she lay back in the armchair and shook with silent laughter.

The children looked at each other. It is not pleasant to be laughed at, especially for something you have never done — but they both felt that Mrs. Pearce would have laughed quite as much, or even more, if they had told her what it really was they had wanted the barrow for.

"Oh, don't go on laughing," said Mavis, creeping close to Mrs. Pearce — "though you are a ducky darling not to be cross any more. And you won't tell, will you?"

"Ah, well — I'll let you off this time. But you'll promise faithful never to do it again, now, won't you?"

"We faithfully won't ever," said both children, earnestly.

"Then off you go to your beds, and I'll dry the things when your Ma's out. I'll press 'em tomorrow morning while I'm waiting for the boys to come in."

"You *are* an angel," said Mavis, embracing her.

"More than you are then, you young limbs," said Mrs. Pearce, returning the embrace. "Now off you go, and get what sleep you can."

It was with a feeling that Fate had not, after all, been unduly harsh with them that Mavis and Francis came down to a very late breakfast.

"Your Ma and Pa's gone off on their bikes," said Mrs. Pearce, bringing in the eggs and bacon — "won't be back till dinner. So I let you have your sleep out. The little 'uns had theirs three hours ago and out on the sands. I told them to let you sleep, though I know they wanted to hear how many shrimps you caught. I lay they expected a barrowful, same as what you did."

"How did you know they knew we'd been out?" Francis asked.

"Oh, the way they was being secret in corners, and looking the old barrow all over was enough to make a cat laugh. Hurry up, now. I've got the washing-up to do — and your things is well-nigh dry."

"You *are* a darling," said Mavis. "Suppose you'd been different, whatever would have become of us?"

"You'd a got your desserts — bed and bread and water, instead of this nice egg and bacon and the sands to play on. So now you know," said Mrs. Pearce.

On the sands they found Kathleen and Bernard, and it really now, in the bright warm sunshine, seemed almost worthwhile to have gone through last night's adventures, if only for the pleasure of telling the tale of them to the two who had been safe and warm and dry in bed all the time.

"Though really," said Mavis, when the tale was told, "sitting here and seeing the tents and the children digging, and the ladies knitting, and the gentlemen smoking and throwing stones, it does hardly seem as though there *could* be any magic. And yet, you know, there was."

"It's like I told you about radium and things," said Bernard. "Things aren't magic because they haven't been found out yet. There's always been Mermaids, of course, only people didn't know it."

"But she talks," said Francis.

"Why not?" said Bernard placidly. "Even parrots do that."

"But she talks English," Mavis urged.

"Well," said Bernard, unmoved, "what would you have had her talk?"

And so, in pretty sunshine, between blue sky and good sands, the adventure of the Mermaid seemed to come to an end, to be now only as a tale that is told. And when the four went slowly home to dinner all were, I think, a little sad that this should be so.

"Let's go around and have a look at the empty barrow," Mavis said; "it'll bring it all back to us, and remind us of what was in it, like ladies' gloves and troubadours."

The barrow was where they had left it, but it was not empty. A very dirty piece of folded paper lay in it, addressed in penciled and uncertain characters

To FRANCE.
To BE OPENED.

Francis opened it and read aloud:

"I went back and she came back and she wants you to come back at ded of nite.
RUBE."

"Well, I shan't go," said Francis.

A voice from the bush by the gate made them all start.

"Don't let on you see me," said the Spangled Boy, putting his head out cautiously.

"You seem very fond of hiding in bushes," said Francis.

"I am," said the boy briefly. "Ain't you going — to see her again, I mean?"

"No," said Francis "I've had enough dead of night to last me a long time."

"You a-going, miss?" the boy asked. "No? You are a half-livered crew. It'll be only me, I suppose."

"You're going, then?"

"Well," said the boy, "what do you think?"

"I should go if I were you," said Bernard impartially.

"No, you wouldn't; not if you were me," said Francis. "You don't know how disagreeable she was. I'm fed up with her. And besides, we simply *can't* get out at dead of night now. Mrs. Pearce'll be on the look out. No — it's no go."

"But you *must* manage it somehow," said Kathleen; "you can't let it drop like this. I shan't believe it was magic at all if you do."

"If you were us, you'd have had enough of magic," said Francis. "Why don't you go yourselves — you and Bernard."

"I've a good mind to," said Bernard unexpectedly. "Only not in the middle of the night, because of my being certain to drop my boots. Would you come, Cathay?"

"You know I wanted to before," said Kathleen reproachfully.

"But how?" the others asked.

"Oh," said Bernard, "we must think about that. I say, you chap, we must get to our dinner. Will you be here after?"

"Yes. I ain't going to move from here. You might bring me a bit of grub with you — I ain't had a bite since yesterday tea-time."

"I say," said Francis kindly, "did they stop your grub to punish you for getting wet?"

"They didn't know nothing about my getting wet," he said darkly. "I didn't never go back to the tents. I've cut my lucky, I 'ave 'ooked it' skedaddled, done a bunk, run away."

"And where are you going?"

"*I* dunno," said the Spangled Boy. "I'm running *from*, not to."

The Mermaid's Home

The parents of Mavis, Francis, Kathleen and Bernard were extremely sensible people. If they had not been, this story could never have happened. They were as jolly as any father and mother you ever met, but they were not always fussing and worrying about their children, and they understood perfectly well that children do not care to be absolutely always under the parental eye. So that, while there were always plenty of good times in which the whole family took part, there were also times when Father and Mother went off together and enjoyed themselves in their own grown-up way, while the children enjoyed themselves in theirs. It happened that on this particular afternoon there was to be a concert at Lymington — Father and Mother were going. The children were asked whether they would like to go, and replied with equal courtesy and firmness.

"Very well then," said Mother, "you do whatever you like best. I should play on the shore, I think, if I were you. Only don't go around the corner of the cliff, because that's dangerous at high tide. It's safe so long as you're within sight of the coast guards. Anyone have any more pie? No — then I think I'll run and dress."

"Mother," said Kathleen suddenly, "may we take some pie and things to a little boy who said he hadn't had anything to eat since yesterday?"

"Where is he?" Father asked.

Kathleen blushed purple, but Mavis cautiously replied, "Outside. I'm sure we shall be able to find him."

"Very well," said Mother, "and you might ask Mrs. Pearce to give you some bread and cheese as well. Now, I must simply fly."

"Cathay and I'll help you, Mother," said Mavis, and escaped the further questioning she saw in her father's eye. The boys had slipped away at the first word of what seemed to be Kathleen's amazing indiscretion about the waiting Rube.

"It was quite all right," Kathleen argued later, as they went up the field, carefully carrying a plate of plum pie and the bread and cheese with not so much care and a certain bundle not carefully at all. "I saw flying in Mother's eye before I spoke. And if you *can* ask leave before you do a thing it's always safer."

"And look here," said Mavis. "If the Mermaid wants to see us we've only got to go down and say 'Sabrina fair,' and she's certain to turn up. If it's just seeing us she wants, and not another deadly night adventure."

Reuben did not eat with such pretty manners as yours, perhaps, but there was no doubt about his enjoyment of the food they had brought, though he only stopped eating for half a second, to answer, "Prime. Thank you," to Kathleen's earnest inquiries.

"Now," said Francis when the last crumb of cheese had disappeared and the last trace of plum juice had been licked from the spoon (a tin one, because, as Mrs. Pearce very properly said, you never know) — "now, look here. We're going straight down to the shore to try and see her. And if you like to come with us we can disguise you."

"What in?" Reuben asked. "I did disguise myself once in a false beard and a green-colored mustache, but it didn't take no one in for a moment, not even the dogs."

"We thought," said Mavis gently, "that perhaps the most complete disguise for you would be girl's clothes — because," she added hastily to dispel the thundercloud on Reuben's brow — "because you're such a manly boy. Nobody would give vent to a moment's suspicion. It would be so very unlike *you*."

"G'a long — " said the Spangled Child, his dignity only half soothed.

"And I've brought you some of my things and some sandshoes of France's, because, of course, mine are just kiddy shoes."

At that Reuben burst out laughing and then hummed: *"Go, flatterer, go, I'll not trust to thy vow,"* quite musically.

"Oh, do you know the *Gypsy Countess*? How jolly!" said Kathleen.

"Old Mother Romaine knew a power of songs," he said, suddenly grave. "Come on, chuck us in the togs."

"You just take off your coat and come out and I'll help you dress up," was Francis's offer.

"Best get a skirt over my kicksies first," said Reuben, "case anyone comes by and recognizes the gypsy cheild. Hand us in the silk attire and jewels have to spare."

They pushed the blue serge skirt and jersey through the branches which he held apart.

"Now the 'at," he said, reaching a hand for it. But the hat was too large for the opening in the bush, and he had to come out of it. The moment he was out the girls crowned him with the big rush-hat, around whose crown a blue scarf was twisted, and Francis and Bernard each seizing a leg, adorned those legs with brown stockings and white sandshoes. Reuben, the spangled runaway from the gypsy camp, stood up among his new friends a rather awkward and quite presentable little girl.

"Now," he said, looking down at his serge skirts with a queer smile, "now we shan't be long."

Nor were they. Thrusting the tin spoon and the pie plate and the discarded boots of Reuben into the kind shelter of the bush they made straight for the sea.

When they got to that pleasant part of the shore which is smooth sand and piled shingle, lying between low rocks and high cliffs, Bernard stopped short.

"Now, look here," he said, "if Sabrina fair turns up trumps I don't mind going on with the adventure, but I won't do it if Kathleen's to be in it."

"It's not fair," said Kathleen; "you said I might."

"Did I ?" — Bernard most handsomely referred the matter to the others.

"Yes, you did," said Francis shortly. Mavis said "Yes," and Reuben clinched the matter by saying, "Why, you up and asked her yourself if she'd go along of you."

"All right," said Bernard calmly. "Then I shan't go myself. That's all."

"Oh, bother," said at least three of the five; and Kathleen said: "I don't see why I should always be out of everything."

"Well," said Mavis impatiently, "after all, there's no danger in just trying to *see* the Mermaid. You promise you won't do anything if Bernard says not — that'll do, I suppose? Though why you should be a slave to him just because he chooses to say you're his particular sister, I don't see. Will *that* do, Bear?"

"I'll promise *anything*," said Kathleen, almost in tears, "if you'll only let me come with you all and see the Mermaid if she turns out to be seeable."

So that was settled.

Now came the question of where the magic words should be said.

Mavis and Francis voted for the edge of the rocks where the words had once already been so successfully spoken. Bernard said, "Why not here where we are?" Kathleen said rather sadly that any place would do as long as the Mermaid came when she was called. But Reuben, standing sturdily in his girl's clothes, said:

"Look 'ere. When you've run away like what I have, least said soonest mended, and out of sight's out of mind. What about caves?"

"Caves are too dry, except at high tide," said Francis. "And then they're too wet. Much."

"Not all caves," Reuben reminded him. "If we was to turn and go up by the cliff path. There's a cave up there. I hid in it t'other day. Quite dry, except in one corner, and there it's as wet as you want — a sort of 'orse trough in the rocks it looks like — only deep."

"Is it seawater?" Mavis asked anxiously. And Reuben said:

"Bound to be, so near the sea and all."

But it wasn't. For when they had climbed the cliff path and Reuben had shown them where to turn aside from it, and had put aside the brambles and furze that quite hid the cave's mouth, Francis saw at once that the water here could not be seawater. It was too far above the line which the waves reached, even in the stormiest weather.

"So it's no use," he explained.

But the others said, "Oh, do let's try, now we *are* here," and they went on into the dusky twilight of the cave.

It was a very pretty cave, not chalk, like the cliffs, but roofed and walled with gray flints such as the houses and churches are built of that you see on the downs near Brighton and East-bourne.

"This isn't an accidental cave, you know," said Bernard importantly; "it's built by the hand of man in distant ages, like Stonehenge and the Cheesewring and Kit's Coty House."

The cave was lighted from the entrance where the sunshine crept faintly through the brambles. Their eyes soon grew used

to the gloom and they could see that the floor of the cave was of
dry white sand, and that along one end was a narrow dark pool
of water. Ferns fringed its edge and drooped their fronds to its
smooth surface — a surface which caught a gleam of light, and
shone whitely; but the pool was very still, and they felt
somehow, without knowing why, very deep.

"It's no good, no earthly," said Francis.

"But it's an awfully pretty cave," said Mavis consolingly.
"Thank you for showing it to us, Reuben. And it's jolly cool. Do
let's rest a minute or two. I'm simply boiling, climbing that cliff
path. We'll go down to the sea in a minute. Reuben could wait
here if he felt safer."

"All right, squattez-vous," said Bernard, and the children sat
down at the water's edge, Reuben still very awkward in his girl's
clothes.

It was very, very quiet. Only now and then one fat drop of
water would fall from the cave's roof into that quiet pool and
just move its surface in a spreading circle.

"It's a ripping place for a hidey-hole," said Bernard, "better
than that old bush of yours, anyhow. I don't believe anybody
knows of the way in."

"I don't think anyone does, either," said Reuben, "because
there wasn't any way in till it fell in two days ago, when I was
trying to dig up a furze root."

"I should hide here if you want to hide," said Bernard.

"I mean to," said Reuben.

"Well, if you're rested, let's get on," Francis said; but
Kathleen urged:

"Do let's say 'Sabrina fair,' first — just to try!" So they said
it — all but the Spangled Child who did not know it —

"Sabrina fair
    Listen where thou art sitting
  Under the glassie, cool..."

There was a splash and a swirl in the pool, and there was the Mermaid herself sure enough. Their eyes had grown used to the dusk and they could see her quite plainly, could see too, that she was holding out her arms to them and smiling so sweetly that it almost took their breath away.

"My cherished preservers," she cried, "my dear, darling, kind, brave, noble, unselfish dears!"

"You're talking to Reuben, in the plural, by mistake, I suppose," said Francis, a little bitterly.

"To him too, of course. But you two most of all," she said, swishing her tail around and leaning her hands on the edge of the pool. "I *am* so sorry I was so ungrateful the other night. I'll tell you how it was. It's in your air. You see, coming out of the water we're very susceptible to aerial influences — and that sort of ungratefulness and, what's the word?"

"Snobbishness," said Francis firmly.

"Is that what you call it? — is most frightfully infectious, and your air's absolutely crammed with the germs of it. That's why I was so horrid. You do forgive me, don't you, dears? And I was so selfish, too — oh, horrid. But it's all washed off now, in the nice clean sea, and I'm as sorry as if it had been my fault, which it really and truly wasn't."

The children said all right, and she wasn't to mind, and it didn't matter, and all the things you say when people say they are sorry, and you cannot kiss them and say, "Right oh," which is the natural answer to such confessions.

"It was very curious," she said thoughtfully, "a most odd experience, that little boy... his having been born of people who had always been rich, really seemed to me to be important. I assure you it did. Funny, wasn't it? And now I want you all to come home with me, and see where I live."

She smiled radiantly at them, and they all said, "Thank you," and looked at each other rather blankly.

"All our people will be unspeakably pleased to see you. We Mer-people are not really ungrateful. You mustn't think that," she said pleadingly.

She looked very kind, very friendly. But Francis thought of the Lorelei. Just so kind and friendly must the Lady of the Rhine have looked to the "sailor in a little skiff" whom he had disentangled from Heine's poem, last term, with the aid of the German dicker. By a curious coincidence and the same hard means, Mavis had, only last term, read of Undine, and she tried not to think that there was any lack of soul in the Mermaid's kind eyes. Kathleen who, by another coincidence, had fed her fancy in English literature on the *Forsaken Merman* was more at ease.

"Do you mean down with you under the sea?" she asked, —

"Where the sea snakes coil and twine,
Dry their mail and bask in the brine,
Where great whales go sailing by,
Sail and sail with unshut eye
Round the world for ever and aye?"

"Well, it's not exactly like that, really" said the Mermaid; "but you'll see soon enough."

This had, in Bernard's ears, a sinister ring.

"Why," he asked suddenly, "did you say you wanted to see us at dead of night?"

"It's the usual time, isn't it?" she asked, looking at him with innocent surprise. "It is in all the stories. You know we have air-stories just as you have fairy stories and water stories — and the rescuer almost always comes to the castle gate at dead of night, on a coal-black steed or a dapple-gray, you know, or a red-roan steed of might; but as there were four of you, besides me and my tail, I thought it more considerate to suggest a chariot. Now, we really ought to be going."

"Which way?" asked Bernard, and everyone held their breath to hear the answer.

"The way I came, of course," she answered, "down here," and she pointed to the water that rippled around her.

"Thank you so very, *very* much," said Mavis, in a voice which trembled a little; "but I don't know whether you've heard that people who go down into the water like that — people like us — without tails, you know — they get drowned."

"Not if they're personally conducted," said the Mermaid. "Of course, we can't be responsible for trespassers, though even with them I don't think anything very dreadful has ever happened. Someone once told me a story about Water Babies. Did you ever hear of that?"

"Yes, but that was a made-up story," said Bernard stolidly.

"Yes, of course," she agreed, "but a great deal of it's quite true, all the same. But you won't grow fins and gills or anything like that. You needn't be afraid."

The children looked at each other, and then all looked at Francis. He spoke.

"Thank you," he said. "Thank you very much, but we would rather not — much rather."

"Oh, nonsense," said the lady kindly. "Look here, it's as easy as easy. I give you each a lock of my hair," she cut off the locks with her shell knife as she spoke, long locks they were and soft. "Look here, tie these round your necks — if I'd had a lock of human hair round my neck I should never have suffered from the dryness as I did. And then just jump in. Keep your eyes shut. It's rather confusing if you don't; but there's no danger."

The children took the locks of hair, but no one regarded them with any confidence at all as lifesaving apparatus. They still hung back.

"You really are silly," said the sea-lady indulgently. "Why did you meddle with magic at all if you weren't prepared to go through with it? Why, this is one of the simplest forms of magic, and the safest. Whatever would you have done if you had happened to call up a fire spirit and had had to go down Vesuvius with a Salamander around your little necks?"

She laughed merrily at the thought. But her laugh sounded a little angry too.

"Come, don't be foolish," she said. "You'll never have such a chance again. And I feel that this air is full of your horrid human microbes — distrust, suspicion, fear, anger, resentment — horrid little germs. I don't want to risk catching them. Come."

"No," said Francis, and held out to her the lock of her hair; so did Mavis and Bernard. But Kathleen had tied the lock of hair around her neck, and she said:

"I *should* have liked to, but I promised Bernard I would not do anything unless he said I might." It was towards Kathleen that the Mermaid turned, holding out a white hand for the lock.

Kathleen bent over the water trying to untie it, and in one awful instant the Mermaid had reared herself up in the water, caught Kathleen in her long white arms, pulled her over the edge of the pool, and with a bubbling splash disappeared with her beneath the dark water.

Mavis screamed and knew it; Francis and Bernard thought they did not scream. It was the Spangled Child alone who said nothing. He had not offered to give back the lock of soft hair. He, like Kathleen, had knotted it around his neck; he now tied a further knot, stepped forward, and spoke in tones which the other three thought the most noble they had ever heard.

"She give me the plum pie," he said, and leaped into the water.

He sank at once. And this, curiously enough, gave the others confidence. If he had struggled — but no — he sank like a stone, or like a diver who means diving and diving to the very bottom.

"She's my special sister," said Bernard, and leaped.

"If it's magic it's all right — and if it isn't we couldn't go back home without her," said Mavis hoarsely. And she and Francis took hands and jumped together.

SHE CAUGHT KATHLEEN IN HER ARMS.

It was not so difficult as it sounds. From the moment of Kathleen's disappearance the sense of magic — which is rather like very sleepy comfort and sweet scent and sweet music that you just can't hear the tune of — had been growing stronger and stronger. And there are some things so horrible that if you can bring yourself to face them you simply *can't* believe that they're true. It did not seem possible — when they came quite close to the idea — that a Mermaid could really come and talk so kindly and then drown the five children who had rescued her.

"It's all right," Francis cried as they jumped.

"I..." He shut his mouth just in time, and down they went.

You have probably dreamed that you were a perfect swimmer? You know the delight of that dream — swimming, which is no effort at all, and yet carries you as far and as fast as you choose. It was like that with the children. The moment they touched the water they felt that they belonged in it — that they were as much at home in water as in air. As they sank beneath the water their feet went up and their heads went down, and there they were swimming downward with long, steady, easy strokes. It was like swimming down a well that presently widened to a cavern. Suddenly Francis found that his head was above water. So was Mavis's.

"All right so far," she said, "but how are we going to get back?"

"Oh, the magic will do that," he answered, and swam faster.

The cave was lighted by bars of phosphorescence placed like pillars against the walls. The water was clear and deeply green and along the sides of the stream were sea anemones and starfish of the most beautiful forms and the most dazzling colors. The walls were of dark squarish shapes, and here and there a white oblong, or a blue and a red, and the roof was of mother-of-pearl which gleamed and glistened in the pale golden radiance of the phosphorescent pillars. It was very beautiful, and the mere pleasure of swimming so finely and easily swept away almost their last fear. This too, went when a voice far ahead called: "Hurry up, France — Come on, Mavis," — and the voice was the voice of Kathleen.

They hurried up, and they came on; and the gleaming soft light grew brighter and brighter. It shone all along the way they had to go, making a path of glory such as the moon makes across the sea on a summer night. And presently they saw that this growing light was from a great gate that barred the waterway in front of them. Five steps led up to this gate, and sitting on it, waiting for them, were Kathleen, Reuben, Bernard and the Mermaid. Only now she had no tail. It lay beside her on the marble steps, just as your stockings lie when you have taken them off; and there were her white feet sticking out from under a dress of soft feathery red seaweed.

They could see it was seaweed though it was woven into a wonderful fabric. Bernard and Kathleen and the Spangled Boy had somehow got seaweed dresses too, and the Spangled Boy was no longer dressed as a girl; and looking down as they scrambled up the steps Mavis and Francis saw that they too, wore seaweed suits — "Very pretty, but how awkward to go home in," Mavis thought.

"Now," said the Mer-lady, "forgive me for taking the plunge. I knew you'd hesitate forever, and I was beginning to feel so cross! That's your dreadful atmosphere! Now, here we are at the door of our kingdom. You do want to come in, don't you? I can bring you as far as this against your will, but not any further. And you can't come any farther unless you trust me absolutely. Do you? Will you? Try!"

"Yes," said the children, all but Bernard, who said stoutly:

"I don't; but I'll try to. I want to."

"If you want to, I think you *do*," said she very kindly. "And now I will tell you one thing. What you're breathing isn't air, and it isn't water. It's something that both water people and air people can breathe."

"The greatest common measure," said Bernard.

"A simple equation," said Mavis.

"Things which are equal to the same thing are equal to each other," said Francis; and the three looked at each other and wondered why they had said such things.

"Don't worry," said the lady, "it's only the influence of the place. This is the Cave of Learning, you know, very dark at the beginning and getting lighter and lighter as you get nearer to the golden door. All these rocks are made of books really, and they exude learning from every crack. We cover them up with anemones and seaweed and pretty things as well as we can, but the learning will leak out. Let us go through the gate or you'll all be talking Sanskrit before we know where we are."

She opened the gate. A great flood of glorious sunlight met them, the solace of green trees and the jeweled grace of bright blossoms. She pulled them through the door, and shut it.

"This is where we live," she said. "Aren't you glad you came?"

The Skies are Falling

As the children passed through the golden doors a sort of swollen feeling which was beginning to make their heads quite uncomfortable passed away, and left them with a curiously clear and comfortable certainty that they were much cleverer than usual.

"I *could* do sums now, and no mistake," Bernard whispered to Kathleen, who replied to the effect that dates no longer presented the slightest difficulty to her.

Mavis and Francis felt as though they had never before known what it was to have a clear brain. They followed the others through the golden door, and then came Reuben, and the Mermaid came last. She had picked up her discarded tail and was carrying it over her arm as you might a shawl. She shut the gate, and its lock clicked sharply.

"We have to be careful, you know," she said, "because of the people in the books. They are always trying to get out of the books that the cave is made of; and some of them are very undesirable characters. There's a Mrs. Fairchild — we've had a great deal of trouble with her, and a person called Mrs. Markham who makes everybody miserable, and a lot of people who think they are being funny when they aren't — dreadful."

The party was now walking along a smooth grassy path, between tall, clipped box hedges — at least they looked like box hedges, but when Mavis stroked the close face of one she found that it was not stiff box, but soft seaweed.

"Are we in the water or not?" said she, stopping suddenly.

"That depends on what you mean by water. Water's a thing human beings can't breathe, isn't it? Well, you are breathing. So this can't be water."

"I see that," said Mavis, "but the soft seaweed won't stand up in air, and it does in water."

"Oh, you've found out, have you?" said the Mermaid. "Well, then, perhaps it is water. Only you see it can't be. Everything's like that down here."

"Once you said you lived in water, and you wanted to be wet," said Mavis.

"Mer-people aren't responsible for what they say in your world. I told you that, you know," the Mermaid reminded them.

Presently they came to a little coral bridge over a stream that flowed still and deep. "But if what we're in is water, what's that?" said Bernard, pointing down.

"Ah, now you're going too deep for me," said the Mermaid, "at least if I were to answer I should go too deep for you. Come on — we shall be too late for the banquet."

"What do you have for the banquet?" Bernard asked; and the Mermaid answered sweetly: "Things to eat."

"And to drink?"

"It's no use," said she; "you can't get at it that way. We drink — but you wouldn't understand."

Here the grassy road widened, and they came onto a terrace of mother-of-pearl, very smooth and shining. Pearly steps led down from it into the most beautiful garden you could invent if you tried for a year and a day with all the loveliest pictures and the most learned books on gardening to help you. But the odd

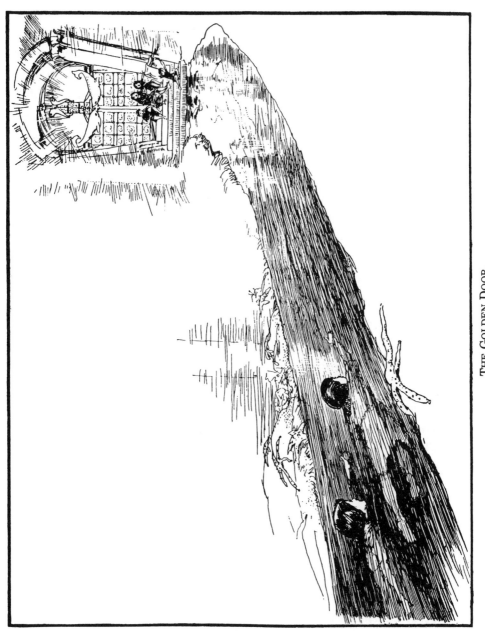

The Golden Door.

thing about it was that when they came to talk it over afterward they never could agree about the shape of the beds, the direction of the walks, the kinds and colors of the flowers, or indeed any single thing about it. But to each it seemed and will always seem the most beautiful garden ever imagined or invented. And everyone saw, beyond a distant belt of trees the shining domes and minarets of very beautiful buildings, and far, faraway there was a sound of music, so faraway that at first they could only hear the music and not the tune. But soon that too was plain, and it was the most beautiful tune in the world.

"Crikey," said Reuben, speaking suddenly and for the first time, "ain't it 'evingly neither. Not arf," he added with decision.

"Now," said the Mermaid, as they neared the belt of trees, "you are going to receive something."

"Oh, thank you," said everybody, and no one liked to add: "What?" — though that simple word trembled on every tongue. It slipped off the tip of Reuben's, indeed, at last, and the Mermaid answered:

"An ovation."

"That's something to do with eggs, I know," said Kathleen. "Father was saying so only the other day."

"There will be no eggs in this," said the Mermaid, "and you may find it a trifle heavy. But when it is over the fun begins. Don't be frightened, Kathleen — Mavis, don't smooth your hair. Ugly untidiness is impossible here. You are about to be publicly thanked by our Queen. You'd rather not? You should have thought of that before. If you will go about doing these noble deeds of rescue you must expect to be thanked. Now, don't forget to bow. And there's nothing to be frightened of."

They passed through the trees and came on a sort of open courtyard in front of a palace of gleaming pearl and gold. There on a silver throne sat the loveliest lady in the world. She wore a starry crown and a gown of green, and golden shoes, and she smiled at them so kindly that they forgot any fear they may have felt. The music ended on a note of piercing sweetness and in the great hush that followed the children felt themselves gently pushed forward to the foot of the throne. All around was a great crowd, forming a circle about the pearly pavement on which they stood.

The Queen rose up in her place and reached toward them the end of her scepter where shone a star like those that crowned her.

"Welcome," she said in a voice far sweeter than the music, "Welcome to our Home. You have been kind, you have been brave, you have been unselfish, and all my subjects do homage to you."

At the word the whole of that great crowd bent toward them like bulrushes in the wind, and the Queen herself came down the steps of her throne and held out her hands to the children.

A choking feeling in their throats became almost unbearable as those kind hands rested on one head after another.

Then the crowd raised itself and stood upright, and someone called out in a voice like a trumpet:

"The children saved one of us — *We die in captivity*. Shout for the children. Shout!"

And a roar like the roar of wild waves breaking on rocks went up from the great crowd that stood all about them. There was a fluttering of flags or handkerchiefs — the children could not tell which — and then the voice of their own Mermaid, saying: "There — that's over. And now we shall have the banquet. Shan't we, Mamma?"

"Yes, my daughter," said the Queen.

So the Mermaid they had rescued was a Queen's daughter!

"I didn't know you were a Princess," said Mavis, as they followed the Queen along a corridor.

"That's why they have made such a fuss, I suppose," said Bernard.

"Oh, no, we should have given the ovation to anyone who had saved any of us from captivity. We love giving ovations. Only we so seldom get the chance, and even ordinary entertaining is difficult. People are so prejudiced. We can hardly ever get anyone to come and visit us. I shouldn't have got you if you hadn't happened to find that cave. It would have been quite impossible for me to give Kathleen that clinging embrace from shallow water. The cave water is so much more buoyant than the sea. I daresay you noticed that."

Yes — they had.

"May we sit next you at the banquet?" Kathleen asked suddenly, "because, you know, it's all rather strange to us."

"Of course, dear," said the sea lady.

"But," said Bernard, "I'm awfully sorry, but I think we ought to go home."

"Oh, don't talk of it," said the Mermaid. "Why, you've only just come."

Bernard muttered something about getting home in time to wash for tea.

"There'll be heaps of time," said Francis impatiently; "don't fuss and spoil everything."

"I'm not fussing," said Bernard, stolid as ever. "I never fuss. But I think we ought to be thinking of getting home."

"Well, think about it then," said Francis impatiently, and turned to admire the clusters of scarlet flowers that hung from the pillars of the gallery.

The banquet was very magnificent, but they never could remember afterward what it was that they ate out of the silver dishes and drank out of the golden cups. They none of them forgot the footmen, however, who were dressed in tight-fitting suits of silver scales, with silver fingerless gloves, and a sort of helmet on that made them look less like people than like fish, as Kathleen said.

"But they *are* fish," said the Princess, opening her beautiful eyes; "they're the Salmoners, and the one behind Mother's chair is the Grand Salmoner. In your country I have heard there are Grand Almoners. We have Grand Salmoners."

"Are all your servants fish?" Mavis asked.

"Of course," said the Princess, "but we don't use servants much except for state occasions. Most of our work is done by the lower orders — electric eels, most of them. We get all the power for our machinery from them."

"How do you do it?" Bernard asked, with a fleeting vision of being some day known as the great man who discovered the commercial value of the electricity obtainable from eels.

"We keep a tank of them," said she, "and you just turn a tap — they're connected up to people's houses — and you connect them with your looms or lathes or whatever you're working. That sets up a continuous current and the eels swim around and around in the current till the work's done. It's beautifully simple."

"It's simply beautiful," said Mavis warmly. "I mean all this," she waved her hand to the row of white arches through which the green of the garden and the blue of what looked like the sky showed plainly. "And you live down here and do nothing but play all day long? How lovely."

"You'd soon get tired of play if you did nothing else," said Bernard wisely. "At least I know I should. Did you ever make a steam engine?" he asked the Princess. "That's what I call work."

"It would be, to me," she said, "but don't you know that work is what you have to do and don't like doing? And play's whatever you want to do. Have some more Andrew Aromaticus."

She made a sign to a Salmoner, who approached with a great salver of fruit. The company were seated by fours and fives and sixes at little tables, such as you see in the dining rooms of the big hotels where people feed who have motors. These little tables are good for conversation.

"Then what *do* you do?" Kathleen asked.

"Well, we have to keep all the rivers flowing, for one thing — the earthly rivers, I mean — and to see to the rain and snow taps, and to attend to the tides and whirlpools, and open the cages where the winds are kept. Oh, it's no easy business being a Princess in our country, I can tell you, whatever it may be in yours. What do your Princesses do? Do they open the wind cages?"

"I... I don't know," said the children. "I think they only open bazaars."

"Mother says they work awfully hard, and they go and see people who are ill in hospitals," Kathleen was beginning, but at this moment the Queen rose and so did everyone else.

"Come," said the Princess, "I must go and take my turn at river-filling. Only Princesses can do the finest sort of work."

"What is the hardest thing you have to do?" Francis asked as they walked out into the garden.

"Keeping the sea out of our kingdom," was the answer, "and fighting the Under Folk. We kept the sea out by trying very hard with both hands, inside our minds. And, of course, the sky helps."

"And how do you fight the Under Folk — and who are they?" Bernard wanted to know.

"Why, the thick-headed, heavy people who live in the deep sea."

"Different from you?" Kathleen asked.

"My dear child!"

"She means," explained Mavis, "that we didn't know there were any other kind of people in the sea except your kind."

"You know much less about us than we do about you," said the Princess. "Of course, there are different nations and tribes, and different customs and dresses and everything. But there are two great divisions down here besides us, the Thick-Heads and the Thin-Skins, and we have to fight both of them. The Thin-Skins live near the surface of the water, frivolous, silly things like nautiluses and flying fish, very pleasant, but deceitful and light-minded. They are very treacherous. The Thick-Heads live in the cold deep dark waters. They are desperate people."

"Do you ever go down there?"

The Princess shuddered.

"No," she said, "but we might have to. If the water ever came into our kingdom they would attack us, and we should have to drive them out; and then we should have to drive them right down to their own kingdom again. It happened once, in my grandfather's time."

"But how on earth," asked Bernard, "did you ever get the water out again?"

"It wasn't on earth, you know," said the Princess, "and the Whales blew a good deal of it out — the Grampuses did their best, but they don't blow hard enough. And the Octopuses finished the work by sucking the water out with their suckers."

"Do you have cats here then?" asked Kathleen, whose attention had wandered, and had only caught a word that sounded like Pussies.

"Only Octopussies," said the Princess. "but then they're eight times as pussy as your dry-land cats."

What Kathleen's attention had wandered to was a tall lady standing on a marble pedestal in the middle of a pool. She held a big vase over her head, and from it poured a thin stream of water. This stream fell in an arch right across the pool into a narrow channel cut in the marble of the square in which they now stood, ran across the square, and disappeared under a dark arch in the face of the rock.

"There," said the Princess, stopping.

"What is it?" asked Reuben, who had been singularly silent.

"This," she said simply, "is the source of the Nile. And of all other rivers. And it's my turn now. I must not speak again till my term of source-service is at an end. Do what you will. Go where you will. All is yours. Only beware that you do not touch the sky. If once profane hands touch the sky the whole heaven is overwhelmed."

She ran a few steps, jumped, and landed on the marble pedestal without touching the lady who stood there already. Then, with the utmost care, so that the curved arc of the water should not be slackened or diverted, she took the vase in her hands and the other lady in her turn leaped across the pool and stood beside the children and greeted them kindly.

"I am Maia. My sister has told me all you did for her," she said; "it was I who pinched your foot," and as she spoke they knew the voice that had said, among the seaweed-covered rocks at Beachfield: "Save her. We die in captivity."

"What will you do?" she asked, "while my sister performs her source-service?"

"Wait, I suppose," said Bernard. "You see we want to know about going home."

"Didn't you fix a time to be recalled?" asked Maia. And when they said no, her beautiful smiling face suddenly looked grave.

"With whom have you left the charge of speaking the spell of recall?"

"I don't know what you mean," said Bernard. "What spell?"

"The one which enabled me to speak to you that day in the shallows," said Maia. "Of course, my sister explained to you that the spell which enables us to come at your call, is the only one by which you can yourselves return."

"She didn't," said Mavis.

"Ah, she is young and impulsive. But no doubt she arranged with someone to speak the spell and recall you?"

"No, she didn't. She doesn't know any land people except us. She told me so," said Kathleen.

"Well, is the spell written anywhere?" Maia asked.

"Under a picture" they told her not knowing that it was also written in the works of Mr. John Milton.

"Then I'm afraid you'll have to wait 'til someone happens to read what is under the picture," said Maia kindly.

"But the house is locked up; there's no one there to read anything," Bernard reminded them.

There was a dismal silence. Then:

"Perhaps burglars will break in and read it," suggested Reuben kindly. "Anyhow, what's the use of kicking up a shine about it? *I* can't see what you want to go back for. It's a little bit of all right here, so it is — I *don't* think. Plucky sight better than anything *I* ever come across. I'm a-goin' to enjoy myself I am, and see all the sights. Miss, there, said we might."

"Well spoken indeed," said Maia, smiling at his earnest face. "That is the true spirit of the explorer."

"But we're not explorers," said Mavis, a little crossly, for her; "and we're not so selfish as you think, either. Mother will be awfully frightened if we're not home to tea. She'll think we're drowned."

"Well, you *are* drowned," said Maia brightly. "At least that's what I believe you land people call it when you come down to us and neglect to arrange to have the spell of return said for you."

"How horrible," said Mavis. "Oh, Cathay," and she clutched her sister tightly.

"But you needn't *stay* drowned," said the Princess. "Someone's sure to say the spell somehow or other. I assure you that this is true; and then you will go home with the speed of an eel."

They felt, somehow, in their bones that this was true, and it consoled them a little. Things which you feel in your bones are most convincing.

"But Mother," said Mavis.

"You don't seem to know much about magic," said Maia pityingly: "the first principle of magic is that time spent in other worlds doesn't count in your own home. No, I see you don't understand. In your home it's still the same time as it was when you dived into the well in the cave."

"But that's hours ago," said Bernard; and she answered:

"I know. But your time is not like our time at all."

"What's the difference?"

"I can't explain," said the Princess. "You can't compare them any more than you can compare a starlight and a starfish. They're quite, quite different. But the really important thing is that your Mother won't be anxious. So now why not enjoy yourselves?"

And all this time the other Princess had been holding up the jar which was the source of all the rivers in all the world.

"Won't she be very tired?" asked Reuben.

"Yes, but suppose all the rivers dried up — and she had to know how people were suffering — that would be something much harder to bear than tiredness. Look in the pool and see what she is doing for the world."

They looked, and it was like a colored cinematograph; and the pictures melted into one another like the old dissolving views that children used to love so before cinematographs were thought of.

They saw the Red Indians building their wigwams by the great rivers — and the beavers building their dams across the little rivers; they saw brown men setting their fish traps by the Nile, and brown girls sending out little golden-lighted love-ships on the Ganges. They saw the stormy splendor of the St.

Lawrence, and the Medway's pastoral peace. Little streams dappled with sunlight and the shadow of green leaves, and the dark and secret torrents that tear through the underworld in caverns and hidden places. They saw women washing clothes in the Seine, and boys sailing boats on the Serpentine. Naked savages dancing in masks beside tropical streams overshadowed by strange trees and flowers that we do not know — and men in flannels and girls in pink and blue, punting in the backwaters of the Thames. They saw Niagara and the Zambesi Falls; and all the time the surface of the pool was smooth as a mirror and the arched stream that was the source of all they saw poured ceaselessly over their heads and fell splashing softly into its little marble channel.

I don't know how long they would have stayed leaning their elbows on the cool parapet and looking down on the changing pictures, but suddenly a trumpet sounded, drums beat, and everyone looked up.

"It's for the review," said Maia, through the rattle of the drums. "Do you care for soldiers?"

"Rather," said Bernard, "but I didn't know you had soldiers."

"We're very proud of our troops," said the Princess. "I am Colonel of the Lobster Battalion, and my sister commands the Crustacean Brigade; but we're not going on parade today."

The sound of drums was drawing nearer. "This way to the parade ground," said the Princess, leading the way. They looked at the review through a big arch, and it was like looking into a very big aquarium.

The first regiment they saw was, as it happened, the 23rd Lobsters.

If you can imagine a Lobster as big as a Guardsman, and rather stouter, you will have some idea of the splendid appearance of this regiment. Only don't forget that Lobsters in their natural regimentals are not red. They wear a sort of steel-blue armor, and carry arms of dreadful precision. They are terrible fellows, the 23rd, and they marched with an air at once proud and confident.

Then came the 16th Swordfish — in uniform of delicate silver, their drawn swords displayed.

The Queen's Own Gurnards were magnificent in pink and silver, with real helmets and spiked collars; and the Boy Scouts — "The Sea Urchins" as they were familiarly called — were the last of the infantry.

Then came Mermen, mounted on Dolphins and Sea Horses, and the Cetacean Regiments, riding on their whales. Each whale carried a squadron.

"They look like great trams going by," said Francis. And so they did. The children remarked that while the infantry walked upright like any other foot soldiers, the cavalry troops seemed to be, with their mounts, suspended in the air about a foot from the ground.

"And that shows it's water," said Bernard.

"No, it doesn't," said Francis.

"Well, a whale's not a bird," said Bernard.

"And there are other things besides air and water," said Francis.

The Household Brigade was perhaps the handsomest. The Grand Salmoner led his silvery soldiers, and the 100th Halibuts were evidently the sort of troops to make the foes of anywhere "feel sorry they were born."

It was a glorious review, and when it was over the children found that they had been quite forgetting their desire to get home.

But as the back of the last Halibut vanished behind the seaweed trees the desire came back with full force. Princess Maia had disappeared. Their own Princess was, they supposed, still performing her source-service.

Suddenly everything seemed to have grown tiresome.

"Oh, I do wish we could go home," said Kathleen. "Couldn't we just find the door and go out?"

"We might *look* for the door," said Bernard cautiously, "but I don't see how we could get up into the cave again."

"We can swim all right, you know," Mavis reminded them.

"I think it would be pretty low down to go without saying good-bye to the Princesses," said Francis. "Still, there's no harm in *looking* for the door."

They did look for the door. And they did not find it. What they did find was a wall — a great gray wall built of solid stones — above it nothing could be seen but blue sky.

"I do wonder what's on the other side," said Bernard; and someone, I will not say which, said: "Let's climb up and see."

It was easy to climb up, for the big stones had rough edges and so did not fit very closely, and there was room for a toe here and a hand there. In a minute or two they were all up, but they could not see down on the other side because the wall was about eight feet thick. They walked toward the other edge, and still they could not see down; quite close to the edge, and still no seeing.

"It isn't sky at all," said Bernard suddenly. "It's a sort of dome — tin I shouldn't wonder, painted to look like sky."

"It can't be," said someone.

"It is though," said Bernard.

"There couldn't be one so big," said someone else.

"But there *is*," said Bernard.

And then someone — I will not tell you who — put out a hand, and, quite forgetting the Princess's warning, touched the sky. That hand felt something as faint and thin as a bubble — and instantly this something broke, and the sea came pouring into the Mer-people's country.

"Now you've done it," said one of those whose hand it wasn't. And there was no doubt about it; the person who owned the hand *had* done it — and done it very thoroughly. It was plain enough now that what they had been living in was not water, and that this was. The first rush of it was terrible — but in less than a moment the whole kingdom was flooded, and then the water became clear and quiet.

The children found no difficulty in breathing, and it was as easy to walk as it is on land in a high wind. They could not run, but they walked as fast as they could to the place where they had left the Princess pouring out the water for all the rivers in all the world.

And as they went, one of them said, "Oh don't, don't tell it was me. You don't know what punishments they may have here."

The others said of course they wouldn't tell. But the one who had touched the sky felt that it was despised and disgraced.

They found the pedestal, but what had been the pool was only part of the enormous sea, and so was the little marble channel.

The Princess was not there, and they began to look for her, more and more anxious and wretched.

"It's all your fault," said Francis to the guilty one who had broken the sky by touching it; and Bernard said, "You shut up, can't you?"

It was a long time before they found their Princess, and when they did find her they hardly knew her. She came swimming towards them, and she was wearing her tail, and a cuirass and helmet of the most beautiful mother-of-pearl — thin scales of it overlapping; and the crest on her helmet was one great pearl, as big as a billiard ball. She carried something over her arm.

"Here you are," she said. "I've been looking for you. The future is full of danger. The water has got in."

"Yes, we noticed that," said Bernard.

THE SEA CAME POURING IN.

And Mavis said: "Please, it was us. We touched the sky."

"Will they punish us?" asked Cathay.

"There are no punishments here," said the pearly Princess gravely, "only the consequences of your action. Our great defense against the Under Folk is that thin blue dome which you have broken. It can only be broken from the inside. Our enemies were powerless to destroy it. But now they may attack us at any moment. I am going to command my troops. Will you come too?"

"Rather," said Reuben, and the others, somewhat less cordially, agreed. They cheered up a little when the Princess went on.

"It's the only way to make you safe. There are four posts vacant on my staff, and I have brought you the uniforms that go with the appointments." She unfolded five tails, and four little pearly coats like her own, with round pearls for buttons, pearls as big as marbles. "Put these on quickly," she said, "they are enchanted coats, given by Neptune himself to an ancestor of ours. By pressing the third button from the top you can render yourself invisible. The third button below that will make you visible again when you wish it, and the last button of all will enable you to become intangible as well as invisible."

"Intangible?" said Cathay.

"Unfeelable, so you're quite safe."

"But there are only four coats," said Francis. "That is so," said the Princess. "One of you will have to take its chance with the Boy Scouts. Which is it to be?"

Each of the children always said, and thought that it meant to say "I will," but somehow or other the person who spoke first was Reuben. The instant the Princess had said "be," Reuben shouted: "Me," adding however almost at once, "please."

"Right," said the Princess kindly, "off with you! The Sea Urchins' barracks are behind that rock. Off with you! Here, don't forget your tail. It enables you to be as comfortable in the water as any fish."

Reuben took the tail and hastened away.

"Now," said the Princess. And they all began putting on their tails. It was like putting both your feet into a very large stocking. Then came the mail coats.

"Don't we have swords?" Francis asked, looking down at his slim and silvery extremity.

"Swords? In the Crustacean Brigade? Never forget, children, that you belong to the Princess's Own Oysters. Here are your weapons. She pointed to a heap of large oyster shells, as big as Roman shields.

"See," she said, "you hold them this way as a rule. A very powerful spring is released when you hold them *that* way."

"But what do you do with it?" Mavis asked.

"Nip the feet of the enemy," said the Princess, "and it holds on. Under Folk have no tails. You wait till they are near a rock; then flip a foe-man's foot with your good weapon, laying the other end on the rock. The oyster shell will at once attach itself to the rock and..."

A terrible shout rang out, and the Princess stopped.

"What is it; oh, what is it?" said the children. And the Princess shuddered:

Again that shout — the most terrible sound the children had ever heard.

"What is it?" they said again.

The Princess drew herself up, as if ashamed of her momentary weakness, and said:

"It is the war cry of the Under Folk."

The Water War

After the sound of that terrible shouting there came silence — that is, there was silence where the children were, but all above they could hear the rush and rustle of a quick arming.

"The war cry of the People of the Depths," said the Princess.

"I suppose, said Kathleen forlornly, "that if they're so near as that all is lost."

"Lost? No, indeed," cried the Princess. "The People of the Depths are very strong, but they are very heavy. They cannot rise up and come to us from the water above. Before they can get in they must scale the wall."

"But they will get over the wall — won't they?"

"Not while one of the Royal Halibuts still lives. The Halibuts have manned the wall; they will keep back the foe. But they won't attack yet. They'll send out their scouts and skirmishers. Till they approach, the Crustacean Brigade can do nothing. It is a hard thing to watch a fight in which you may not share. I must apologize for appointing you to such an unsatisfactory position."

"Thank you, *we* don't mind," said Cathay hastily. "What's that?"

It was a solid, gleaming sheet of silver that rose above them like a great carpet — which split and tore itself into silver threads.

"It is the Swordfish Brigade," said the Princess. "We could swim up a little and watch them, if you're not afraid. You see, the first attack will probably be delivered by one of their Shark regiments. The 7th Sharks have a horrible reputation. But our brave Swordfish are a match for them," she added proudly.

The Swordfish, who were slowly swimming to and fro above, seemed to stiffen as though to meet some danger at present unseen by the others. Then, with a swift, silent, terrible movement, the Sharks rushed on the noble defenders of Merland.

The Swordfish with their deadly weapons were ready — and next moment all the water was a wild whirl of confused conflict. The Sharks fought with a sort of harsh, rough courage, and the children, who had drawn away to a little distance, could not help admiring their desperate onslaught. But the Sword-fish were more than their match. With more skill, and an equally desperate gallantry, they met and repulsed the savage onslaught of the Sharks.

Shoals of large, calm Cod swept up from the depths, and began to shoulder the dead Sharks sideways toward the water above the walls — the dead Sharks and, alas! many a brave, dead Swordfish too. For the victory had not been a cheap one.

The children could not help cheering as the victorious Swordfish re-formed.

"Pursuit is unnecessary," said the Princess. "The Sharks have lost too heavily to resume the attack."

A Shark in terror-stricken retreat passed close by her, and she clipped its tail with her oyster shell.

The Shark turned savagely, but the Princess with one tail-swish was out of danger, pushing the children before her outspread arms, and the Shark began to sink, still making vain efforts to pursue them.

THE SWORDFISH BRIGADE.

"The shell will drag him down," said the Princess; "and now I must go and get a fresh shield. I wish I knew where the next attack would be delivered."

They sank slowly through the water.

"I wonder where Reuben is?" said Bernard.

"Oh, he's quite safe," said the Princess. "The Boy Scouts don't go outside the walls — they just do a good turn for anybody who wants it, you know — and help the kind Soles to look after the wounded."

They had reached the great flooded garden again and turned toward the Palace, and as they went a Sea Urchin shell suddenly rose from behind one of the clipped hedges — a Sea Urchin shell and behind it a long tail.

The shell was raised, and the face under it was Reuben's.

"Hi, Princess!" he shouted. "I've been looking for you everywhere. We've been scouting. I got a lot of seaweed, and they thought I was nothing but seaweed; and so I got quite close to the enemy."

"It was very rash," said the Princess severely.

"The others don't think so," he said, a little hurt. "They began by saying I was only an irregular Sea Urchin, because I've got this jolly tail" — he gave it a merry wag — "and they called me Spatangus, and names like that. But they've made me their General now — General Echinus. I'm a regular now, and no mistake, and what I was going to say is the enemy is going to attack the North Tower in force in half an hour."

"You good boy," said the Princess. I do believe if it hadn't been for his Sea Urchin's uniform she would have kissed him. "You're splendid. You're a hero. If you could do it safely — there's heaps of seaweed — could you find out if there's any danger from the Book People? You know — the ones in the cave. It's always been our fear that they might attack *too*: and if they did — well, I'd rather be the slave of a Shark than of Mrs.

Fairchild." She gathered an armful of seaweed from the nearest tree, and Reuben wrapped himself in it and drifted off — looking less like a live Boy Scout than you could believe possible.

The defenders of Merland, now acting on Reuben's information, began to mass themselves near the North Wall.

"Now is our time," said the Princess. "We must go along the tunnel, and when we hear the sound of their heavy feet shaking the flow of ocean we must make sallies, and fix our shell shields in their feet. Major, rally your men."

A tall Merchild in the Crustacean uniform blew a clear note, and the soldiers of the Crustacean Brigade, who having nothing particular to do had been helping anyone and everyone as best they could, which is the way in Merland, though not in Europe, gathered about their officers.

When they were all drawn up before her, the Princess addressed her troops.

"My men," she said, "we have been suddenly plunged into war. But it has not found us unprepared. I am proud to think that my regiments are ready to the last pearl-button. And I know that every man among you will be as proud as I am that our post is, as tradition tells us it has always been, the post of danger. We shall go out into the depths of the sea to fight the enemies of our dear country, and to lay down our lives, if need be, for that country's sake."

The soldiers answered by cheers, and the Princess led the way to one of those little buildings, like Temples of Flora in old pictures, which the children had noticed in the gardens. At the order given a sergeant raised a great stone by a golden ring embedded in it and disclosed a dark passage leading underground.

A splendid captain of Cockles, six feet high if he was an inch, with a sergeant and six men, led the way. Three Oyster officers followed, then a company of Oysters, the advance guard. At the head of the main body following were the Princess and her Staff. As they went the Princess explained why the tunnel was so long and sloped so steeply.

"You see," she said, "the inside of our wall is only about ten feet high, but it goes down on the other side for forty feet or more. It is built on a hill. Now, I don't want you to feel obliged to come out and fight. You can stay inside and get the shields ready for us to take. We shall keep on rushing back for fresh weapons. Of course, the tunnel's much too narrow for the Under Folk to get in, but they have their regiment of highly trained Sea Serpents, who, of course, can make themselves thin and worm through anything."

"Cathay doesn't like serpents," said Mavis anxiously.

"You needn't be afraid," said the Princess. "They're dreadful cowards. They know the passage is guarded by our Lobsters. They won't come within a mile of the entrance. But the main body of the enemy will have to pass quite close. There's a great sea mountain, and the only way to our North Tower is in the narrow ravine between that mountain and Merland."

The tunnel ended in a large rocky hall with the armory, hung with ten thousand gleaming shields, on the one side, and the guardroom crowded with enthusiastic Lobsters on the other. The entrance from the sea was a short, narrow passage, in which stood two Lobsters in their beautiful dark coats of mail.

Since the moment when the blue sky that looked first so like sky and then so like painted tin had, touched, confessed itself to be a bubble — confessed too, in the most practical way, by bursting and letting the water into Merland — the children had been carried along by the breathless rush of preparations for the invasion, and the world they were now in had rapidly increased in reality, while their own world, in which till today they had always lived, had been losing reality at exactly the same rate as that by which the new world gained it. So it was that when the Princess said:

"You needn't go out and attack the enemy unless you like," they all answered, in some astonishment:

"But we *want* to."

"That's all right," said the Princess. "I only wanted to see if they were in working order."

"If what were?"

"Your coats. They're coats of valor, of course."

"I think I could be brave without a coat," said Bernard, and began to undo his pearl buttons.

"Of course you could," said the Princess. "In fact, you must be brave to begin with, or the coat couldn't work. It would be no good to a coward. It just keeps your natural valor warm and your wits cool."

"It makes you braver," said Kathleen suddenly. "At least I hope it's me — but I expect it's the coat. Anyhow, I'm glad it does. Because I do want to be brave. Oh, Princess!"

"Well ?" said the Princess, gravely, but not unkindly, "what is it?"

Kathleen stood a moment, her hands twisting in each other and her eyes downcast. Then in an instant she had unbuttoned and pulled off her coat of pearly mail and thrown it at the Princess's feet.

"I'll do it without the coat," she said, and drew a long breath.

The others looked on in silence, longing to help her, but knowing that no one could help her now but herself.

"It was me," said Kathleen suddenly, and let go a deep breath of relief. "It was me that touched the sky and let in the water; and I am most frightfully sorry, and I know you'll never forgive me. But — "

"Quick," said the Princess, picking up the coat, "get into your armor; it'll prevent your crying." She hustled Kathleen into the coat and kept her arms around her. "Brave girl," she whispered. "I'm glad you did it without the coat." The other three thought it polite to turn away. "Of course," the Princess added, "I knew — but you didn't know I knew."

"How did you know?" said Kathleen.

"By your eyes," said the Princess, with one last hug; "they're quite different now. Come, let us go to the gate and see if any of our Scouts are signaling."

The two Lobster sentries presented claws as the Princess passed with her Staff through the narrow arch and onto the sandy plain of the sea bottom. The children were astonished to find that they could see quite plain a long way through the water — as far as they could have seen in air, and the view was very like one kind of land view. First, the smooth flat sand dotted with copses of branching seaweed — then woods of taller treelike weeds with rocks shelving up and up to a tall, rocky mountain. This mountain sent out a spur, then ran along beside the Merkingdom and joined the rock behind it; and it was along the narrow gorge so formed that the Under Folk were expected to advance. There were balls of seaweed floating in the air — at least, it really now had grown to seem like air, though, of course, it was water — but no signs of Scouts.

Suddenly the balls of seaweed drew together and the Princess murmured, "I thought so," as they formed into orderly lines, sank to the ground, and remained motionless for a moment, while one ball of seaweed stood in front of them.

"It's the Boy Scouts," she said. "Your Reuben is giving them their orders."

It seemed that she was right, for next moment the balls of seaweed drifted away in different directions, and the one who had stood before them drifted straight to the arch where the Princess and the children stood. It drifted in, pulled off its seaweed disguise, and was, in effect, Reuben.

"We've found out something more, your Highness," he said, saluting the Princess. "The vanguard are to be Sea Horses; you know, not the little ones, but the great things they have in the depths."

"No use our attacking the horses," said the Princess. "They're as hard as ice. Who rides them?"

"The First Dipsys," said Reuben. "They're the young Under Folk who want to cut a dash. They call them the Forlorn Hopers, for short."

"Have they got armor?"

"No — that's their swank. They've no armor but their natural scales. Those look thick enough, though. I say, Princess, I suppose we Sea Urchins are free to do exactly as we choose?"

"Yes," said the Princess, "unless orders are given."

"Well, then — my idea is that the Lobsters are the fellows to tackle the Sea Horses. Hold on to their tails, see? They can't hurt the Lobsters because they can't get at their own tails."

"But when the Lobsters let go?" said the Princess.

"The Lobsters wouldn't let go till they had driven back the enemy," said the Lobster Captain, saluting. "Your Highness, may I ask if you propose to take this Urchin's advice?"

"Isn't it good?" she asked.

"Yes, your Highness," the Lobster Captain answered, "but it's impertinent."

"I am the best judge of that," said the Princess gently; "remember that these are noble volunteers, who are fighting for us of their own free will."

The Lobster saluted and was silent.

"I cannot send the Lobsters," said the Princess, "we need them to protect the gate. But the Crabs — "

"Ah, Highness, let us go," pleaded the Lobster Captain.

"The Crabs cannot keep the gate," said the Princess kindly. "You know they are not narrow enough. Francis, will you be my aide-de-camp and take a message to the Queen?"

THE FIRST DIPSYS.

"May I go, too?" asked Mavis.

"Yes. But we must deliver a double assault. If the Crabs attack the Horses, who will deal with the riders?"

"I have an idea about that too," said Reuben.

"If we could have some good heavy shoving regiment — and someone sharp to finish them off. The Swordfish, perhaps?"

"You are a born general," the Princess said; "but you don't quite know our resources. The United Narwhals can do the shoving, as you call it — and their horns are sharp and heavy. Now" — she took a smooth white chalkstone from the seafloor, and a ready Lobster brought her a sharpened haddock bone. She wrote quickly, scratching the letters deep on the chalk. "Here," she said, "take this to the Queen. You will find her at Headquarters at the Palace yard. Tell her everything. I have only asked for the two regiments; you must explain the rest. I don't suppose there'll be any difficulty in getting through our lines, but, if there should be, the password is 'Glory' and the countersign is 'or Death.' And hurry, hurry, hurry for your lives!"

Never before had Mavis and Francis felt anything like the glow of excitement and importance which warmed them as they went up the long tunnel to take the message to the Queen.

"But where is the Palace?" Mavis said, and they stopped, looking at each other.

"I'll show you, please," said a little voice behind them. They turned quickly to find a small, spruce, gentlemanly Mackerel at their heels. "I'm one of the Guides," it said. "I felt sure you'd need me. This way, sir, please," and it led the way across the gardens in and out of the clumps of trees and between the seaweed hedges till they came to the Palace. Rows and rows of soldiers surrounded it, all waiting impatiently for the word of command that should send them to meet the enemies of their country.

"Glory, said the gentlemanly Mackerel, as he passed the outposts.

"Or Death," replied the sentinel Sea bream.

The Queen was in the courtyard, in which the children had received their ovation — so short a time ago, and yet how long it seemed. Then the courtyard had been a scene of the calm and charming gaiety of a nation at peace; now it was full of the ardent, intense inactivity of waiting warriors. The Queen in her gleaming coral armor met them as the password opened a way to her through the close-packed ranks of the soldiers. She took the stone and read it, and with true royal kindness she found time, even at such a moment, for a word of thanks to the messengers.

"See the Narwhals start," she added, "and then back to your posts with all speed. Tell your commanding officer that so far the Book People have made no sign, but the golden gate is strongly defended by the King's Own Cod, and — "

"I didn't know there was a King," said Francis.

The Queen looked stern, and the Mackerel guide jerked Francis's magic coattail warningly and whispered "Hush!"

"The King," said the Queen quietly, "is no more. He was lost at sea."

When the splendid steady column of Narwhals had marched off to its appointed place the children bowed to the Queen and went back to their posts.

"I'm sorry I said anything," said Francis to the Mackerel, "but I didn't know. Besides, how can a Mer-king be lost at sea?"

"Aren't your Kings lost on land?" asked the Mackerel, "or if not kings, men quite as good? What about explorers?"

"I see," said Mavis; "and doesn't anyone know what has become of him?"

"No," said the Mackerel; "he has been lost for a very long time. We fear the worst. If he were alive he would have come back. We think the Under Folk have him. They bewitch prisoners so that they forget who they are. Of course, there's the antidote. Every uniform is made with a little antidote pocket just over the heart." He put his fin inside his scales and produced a little golden case, just like a skate's egg. "You've got them too, of course," he added. "If you are taken prisoner swallow the contents at once."

"But if you forget who you are," said Francis, "don't you forget the antidote?"

"No charm," the Mackerel assured him, "is strong enough to make one forget one's counter-charm."

And now they were back at the Lobster-guarded gate. The Princess ran to meet them.

"What a time you've been," she said. "Is all well? Have the Narwhals taken up their position?"

Satisfied on this point, she led the children up a way long and steep to a window in the wall whence they could look down on the ravine and see the advance of the foe. The Narwhals were halted about halfway up the ravine, where it widened to a sort of amphitheater. Here, among the rocks, they lay in ambush, waiting for the advance of the foe.

"If it hadn't been for you, Reuben," said the Princess, as they leaned their elbows on the broad rocky ledge of the window, "they might easily have stormed the North Tower — we should not have been ready — all our strongest defenses were massed on the south side. It was there they attacked last time, so the history books tell us."

And now a heavy, thundering sound, faint yet terrible, announced the approach of the enemy — and far away across the sea plain something could be seen moving. A ball of seaweed seemed to drift up the ravine.

"A Sea Urchin gone to give the alarm," said the Princess; "what splendid things Boy Scouts are. We didn't have them in

the last war. My dear father only invented them just before—"
She paused and sighed. "Look," she said.

The enemy's heavy cavalry were moving in a solid mass
toward Merland — the great Sea Horses, twenty feet long, and
their great riders who must have been eight or ten feet high,
came more and more quickly, heading to the ravine. The riders
were the most terrible beings the children had ever seen.
Clothed from head to feet in closely fitting scales, with large
heads, large ears, large mouths and blunt noses and large,
blind-looking eyes, they sat each erect on his armored steed, the
long harpoons swaying lightly in their enormous hands.

The Sea Horses quickened their pace — and a noise like a
hoarse trumpet rang out.

"They are sounding the charge," said the Princess; and as she
spoke the Under Folk charged at the ravine, in a determined,
furious onrush.

"Oh, no one can stand up against that — they can't," said
Cathay, in despair.

From the window they could see right down onto the amphitheater, where the Narwhals were concealed.

On came the Sea Cavalry — so far unresisted — but as they
neared the ambush bunches of seaweed drifted in the faces of
the riders. They floundered and strove to push away the clinging
stuff — and as they strove the Narwhals made their sortie —
drove their weight against the riders and hurled them from their
horses, and front the covers of the rocks the Crabs advanced
with an incredible speed and caught the tails of the Sea Horses
in their inexorable claws. The riders lay on the ground. The
horses were rearing and prancing with fear and pain as the
clouds of seaweed, each with a prickly Sea Urchin in it, flung
themselves against their faces. The riders stood up, fighting to
the last; but the harpoons were no match for the Narwhal's
horns.

"Come away," said the Princess.

Already the Sea Horses, urged by the enormous Crabs, were retreating in the wildest disorder, pursued by Narwhals and harassed by Sea Urchins.

The Princess and the children went back to the Lobster sentries.

"Repulsed," said the Princess, "with heavy loss" — and the Lobsters cheered.

"How's that, Princess?" said a ball of seaweed, uncurling itself at the gate and presenting the familiar features of Reuben.

"How is it?" she said. "It is Victory. And we owe it to you. But you're wounded?"

"Only a scratch," said Reuben; "harpoon just missed me."

"Oh, Reuben, you are a hero," said Cathay.

"Get along, you silly," he answered gracefully.

The Book People

Even in the midst of war there are intervals for refreshments. Our own soldiers, no matter how fierce, must eat to live, and the same is the case with the submarine regiments. The Crustacean Brigade took advantage of the lull in hostilities which followed the defeat of the Sea Horses to march back to the Palace and have a meal. A very plain meal it was too, and very different from the "Banquet of Ovations," as Cathay pointed out afterward. There were no prettily spread tables decorated with bunches of seaweed, no plates or knives or forks. The food was passed around by hand, and there was one drinking horn (a sea cow's horn) to every six soldiers. They all sat on the ground as you do at a picnic, and the Queen came and spoke a few hurried words to them when on her way to strengthen the defenses of the golden gate. And, as I said, the food was plain. However, everyone had enough to eat, which was the main thing. Baskets of provisions were sent down to the Lobsters' guardroom.

"It is important," said Princess Freia, "that our men should be on the spot in case they are needed, and the same with the dinner. I shall go down with the provisions and keep their hearts up.

"Yes, dear, do," said the Princess Maia; "but don't do anything rash. No sorties now. You Lobsters are so terribly

brave. But you know Mother said you weren't to. Ah me! War is
a terrible thing! What a state the rivers will get into with all
this water going on, and the winds all loose and doing as they
like. It's horrible to think about. It will take ages to get things
straight again."

(Her fears were only too well-founded. All this happened last
year — and you know what a wet summer *that* was.)

"I know, dear," said Freia; "but I know now who broke the
sky, and it is very, very sorry — so we won't rub it in, will we?"

"I didn't mean to," said Maia, smiling kindly at the children,
and went off to encourage her Lobsters.

"And now," said Francis, when the meal was over, "what are
we going to do next ?"

"We can't do anything but wait for news," said the Princess.
"Our Scouts will let us know soon enough. I only hope the Book
People won't attack us at the same time as the Under Folk.
That's always the danger."

"How could they get in?" Mavis asked.

"Through the golden door," said the Princess. "Of course, they
couldn't do anything if we hadn't read the books they're in.
That's the worst of Education. We've all read such an awful lot,
and that unlocks the books and they can come out if anyone
calls them. Even our fish are intolerably well read — except the
Porpoises, dear things, who never could read anything. That's
why the golden door is guarded by them, of course."

"If not having read things is useful," said Mavis, "we've read
almost nothing. Couldn't we help guard the door?"

"The very thing," said the Princess joyously; "for you possess
the only weapon that can be used against these people or
against the authors who created them. If you can truthfully say
to them, 'I never heard of you,' your words become a deadly
sword that strikes at their most sensitive spot."

"What spot?" asked Bernard. And the Princess answered, "Their vanity."

So the little party went toward the golden door and found it behind a thick wall of Porpoises. Incessant cries came from beyond the gates, and to every cry they answered like one Porpoise, "We never heard of you. You can't come in. You can't come in. We never heard of you."

"We shan't be any good here," said Bernard, among the thick, rich voices of the Porpoises. "They can keep anyone back."

"Yes," said the Princess; "but if the Book Folk look through the gate and see that they're only Porpoises their wounded vanity will heal, and they'll come on as strongly as ever. Whereas if they did find human beings who have never heard of them the wounds ought to be mortal. As long as you are able truthfully to say that you don't know them they can't get in."

"Reuben would be the person for this," said Francis. "I don't believe he's read anything."

"Well, we haven't read much," said Cathay comfortably; "at least, not about nasty people."

"I wish I hadn't," sighed the Princess through the noise of the voices outside the gate. "I know them all. You hear that cold squeak? That's Mrs. Fairchild. And that short, sharp, barking sound — that's Aunt Fortune. The sort of growl that goes on all the time is Mr. Murdstone, and that icy voice is Rosamund's mother — the one who was so hateful about the purple jar."

"I'm afraid we know some of those," said Mavis.

"Then be careful not to say you don't. There are heaps you don't know — John Knox and Machiavelli and Don Diego and Tippoo Sahib and Sally Brass and — I must go back. If anything should happen, fling your arms round the nearest Porpoise and trust to luck. These Book People can't kill — they can only stupefy."

"But how do you know them all?" Mavis asked. "Do they often attack you?"

"No, only when the sky falls. But they always howl outside the gate at the full moon."

So saying she turned away and disappeared in the crowd of faithful Porpoises.

And outside the noise grew louder and the words more definite.

"I am Mrs. Randolph. Let me in!"

"I am good Mrs. Brown. Let me in!"

"I am Eric, or Little by Little. I *will* come in!"

"I am Elsie, or Like a Little Candle. Let me in — let me in!"

"I am Mrs. Markham."

"I am Mrs. Squeers."

"I am Uriah Heep."

"I am Montdidier."

"I am King John."

"I am Caliban."

"I am the Giant Blunderbore."

"I am the Dragon of Wantley."

And they all cried, again and again: "Let us in! Let me in! Let me in!"

The strain of listening for the names and calling out "I don't know you!" when they didn't, and saying nothing when they did, became almost unbearable. It was like that horrid game with the corners of the handkerchief, "Hold fast" and "Let loose," and you have to remember to do the opposite. Sooner or later an accident is bound to happen, and the children felt a growing conviction that it would be *sooner*.

"What will happen if they do get in?" Cathay asked a neighboring Porpoise.

"Can't say, miss, I'm sure," it answered.

"But what will you do?"

"Obstruct them in the execution of our duty," it answered. "You see, miss, they can't kill; they can only stupefy, and they can't stupefy us, 'cause why? We're that stupid already we can't hold no more. That's why they trust us to defend the golden gate," it added proudly.

The babel of voices outside grew louder and thicker, and the task of knowing when to say "I don't know you," and so wound the vanity of the invaders, grew more and more difficult. At last the disaster, foreseen for some time, with a growing plainness, came upon them.

"I am the Great Seal," said a thick, furry voice.

"I don't know you," cried Cathay.

"You do — he's in history. James the Second dropped him in the Thames," said Francis. "Yes, you've done it again."

"Shut up," said Bernard.

The last two remarks were made in a deep silence, broken only by the heavy breathing of the Porpoises. The voices behind the golden gate had died down and ceased. The Porpoises massed their heavy bulk close to the door.

"Remember the Porpoises," said Francis. "Don't forget to hold onto a Porpoise."

Four of these amiable if unintellectual creatures drew away from their companions, and one came to the side of each child.

Every eye was fixed on the golden door, and then slowly — very slowly, the door began to open. As it opened it revealed the crowd that stood without — cruel faces, stupid faces, crafty faces, sullen faces, angry faces, not a single face that you ever could wish to see again.

Then slowly, terribly, without words, the close ranks of the Book People advanced. Mrs. Fairchild, Mrs. Markham, and Mrs. Barbauld led the van. Closely following came the Dragon of Wantley, the Minotaur, and the Little Man that Sintram knew. Then came Mr. Murdstone, neat in a folded white neckcloth, and clothes as black as his whiskers. Miss Murdstone was with him, every bead of her alight with gratified malice. The children found that they knew, without being told, the name of each foe now advancing on them. Paralyzed with terror, they watched the slow and terrible advance. It was not till Eric, or Little by Little, broke the silence with a whoop of joy and rushed upon them that they remembered their own danger, and clutched the waiting Porpoises. Alas! it was too late. Mrs. Markham had turned a frozen glare upon them, Mrs. Fairchild had wagged an admonitory forefinger, wave on wave of sheer stupidity swept over them, and next moment they lost consciousness and sank, each with his faithful Porpoise, into the dreamless sleep of the entirely unintelligent. In vain the main body of the Porpoises hurled themselves against the intruders; their heroism was fruitless. Overwhelmed by the heavy truisms wielded by the enemy, they turned and fled in disorder, and the conquering army entered Merland.

Francis was the first to recover consciousness. The Porpoise to which he had clung was fanning him with its fin, and imploring him, for its sake, to look up, to speak.

"All right, old chap," said Francis. "I must have fallen asleep. Where are the others?"

They were all there, and the devoted Porpoises quickly restored them to consciousness.

The four children stood up and looked at each other.

"I wish Reuben was here," said Cathay. "He'd know what to do."

"He wouldn't know any more than we do," said Francis haughtily.

"We *must* do *something*," said Mavis. "It's our fault again."

"It's mine," said Cathay, "but I couldn't help it."

"If you hadn't, one of us would have," said Bernard, seeking to console. "I say, why do only the nasty people come out of the books?"

BOOK HORRORS.

"I know that," said his Porpoise, turning his black face eagerly toward them. "The stupidest people can't help knowing *something*. The Under Folk get in and open the books — at least, they send the Bookworms in to open them. And, of course, they only open the pages where the enemies are quartered."

"Then — " said Bernard looking at the golden gate, which swung open, its lock hanging broken and useless.

"Yes," said Mavis, "we could, couldn't we? Open the other books, we mean!" She appealed to her Porpoise.

"Yes," it said, "perhaps you could. Human children can open books, I believe. Porpoises can't. And Mer-people can't open the books in the Cave of Learning, though they can unlock them. If they want to open them they have to get them from the Public Mer Libraries. I can't help knowing that," it added. The Porpoises seemed really ashamed of not being thoroughly stupid.

"Come on," said Francis, "we'll raise an army to fight these Book People. Here's something we can do that *isn't* mischief."

"You shut up," said Bernard, and thumping Cathay on the back told her to never mind.

They went toward the golden gate.

"I suppose all the nasty people are out of the books by now?" Mavis asked her Porpoise, who followed her with the close fidelity of an affectionate little dog.

"*I* don't know," it said, with some pride. "I'm stupid, I am. But I can't help knowing that no one can come out of books unless they're called. You've just got to tap on the back of the book and call the name and then you open it, and the person comes out. At least, that's what the Bookworms do, and I don't see why you should be different."

What *was* different, it soon appeared, was the water in the stream in the Cave of Learning, which was quite plainly still water in some other sense than that in which what they were in was water. That is, they could not walk in it; they had to swim.

The cave seemed dark, but enough light came from the golden gate to enable them to read the titles of the books when they had pulled away the seaweed which covered many of them. They had to hold on to the rocks — which were books — with one hand, and clear away the seaweed with the other.

You can guess the sort of books at which they knocked — Kingsley and Shakespeare and Marryat and Dickens, Miss Alcott and Mrs. Ewing, Hans Andersen and Stevenson, and Mayne Reid — and when they had knocked they called the name of the hero whose help they desired, and "Will you help us," they asked, "to conquer the horrid Book People, and drive them back to cover?"

And not a hero but said, "Yes, indeed we will, with all our hearts."

And they climbed down out of the books, and swam up to the golden gate and waited, talking with courage and dignity among themselves, while the children went on knocking at the backs of books — which are books' front doors — and calling out more and more heroes to help in the fight.

Quentin Durward and Laurie were the first to come out, then Hereward and Amyas and Will Cary, David Copperfield, Rob Roy, Ivanhoe, Caesar and Anthony, Coriolanus and Othello; but you can make the list for yourselves. They came forth, all alive and splendid, with valor and the longing to strike once more a blow for the good cause, as they had been used to do in their old lives.

"These are enough," said Francis, at last. "We ought to leave some, in case we want more help later."

You see for yourselves what a splendid company it was that swam to the golden gate — there was no other way than swimming, except for Perseus — and awaited the children. And when the children joined them — rather nervous at the thought of the speeches they would have to make to their newly recruited regiment — they found that there was no need of speeches. The faithful Porpoises had not been too stupid to explain the simple facts of danger and rescue.

It was a proud moment for the children when they marched toward the Palace at the head of the band of heroes whom they had pressed into the service of the Merland. Between the clipped seaweed hedges they went, and along the paths paved with pearl and marble, and so, at last, drew near the Palace. They gave the watchword "Glory."

"Or Death," said the sentry. And they passed on to the Queen.

"We've brought a reinforcement," said Francis, who had learned the word from Quentin Durward as they came along. And the Queen gave one look at her reinforcement's faces and said simply:

"We are saved."

The horrible Book People had not attacked the Palace; they had gone furtively through the country killing stray fish and destroying any beautiful thing they happened to find. For these people hate beauty and happiness. They were now holding a meeting in the Palace gardens, near the fountain where the Princesses had been wont to do their source-service, and they were making speeches like mad. You could hear the dull, flat murmur of them even from the Palace. They were the sort of people who love the sound of their own silly voices.

The newcomers were ranged in orderly ranks before the Queen, awaiting her orders. It looked like a pageant or a fancy-dress parade. There was St. George in his armor, and Joan of Arc in hers — heroes in plumed hats and laced shirts, heroes in ruffs and doublets — brave gentlemen of England, gallant gentlemen of France. For all the differences in their dress, there was nothing motley about the band which stood before the Queen. Varied as they were in dress and feature, they had one quality in common, which marked them as one company. The same light of bravery shone on them all, and became them like a fine uniform.

"Will you," the Queen asked of their leader — a pale, thin-faced man in the dress of a Roman — "will you do just as you think best? I would not presume," she added, with a kind of proud humility, "to teach the game of war to Caesar."

"Oh, Queen," he answered, "these brave men and I will drive back the intruders, but, having driven them back, we must ourselves return through those dark doors which we passed when your young defenders called our names. We will drive back the *men* — and by the look of them 'twill be an easy task. But Caesar wars not with women, and the women on our side are few, though each, I doubt not, has the heart of a lioness."

He turned towards Joan of Arc with a smile and she gave him back a smile as bright as the sword she carried.

"How many women are there among you?" the Queen asked, and Joan answered:

"Queen Boadicea and Torfrida and I are but three."

"But we three," cried Torfrida, "are a match for three hundred of such women as those. Give us but whips instead of swords, and we will drive them like dogs to their red and blue cloth-bound kennels."

"I'm afraid," said the Queen, "they'd overcome you by sheer weight. You've no idea how heavy they are." And then Kathleen covered herself with glory by saying, "Well, but what about Amazons?"

"The very thing," said Caesar kindly. "Would you mind running back? You'll find them in the third book from the corner where the large purple starfish is; you can't mistake it."

The children tore off to the golden gate, rushed through it, and swam to the spot where, unmistakably, the purplish starfish spread its violet rays. They knocked on the book, and Cathay, by previous arrangement, called out —

"Come out, please, Queen of the Amazons, and bring all your fighting ladies."

Then out came a very splendid lady in glorious golden armor. "You'd better get some boats for us," she said, standing straight and splendid on a ledge of rock, "enough to reach from here to the gate, or a bridge. There are all these things in Caesar's books. I'm sure he wouldn't mind your calling them out. We must not swim, I know, because of getting our bowstrings wet."

So Francis called out a bridge, and when it was not long enough to reach the golden gate he called another. And then the Queen called her ladies, and out came a procession, which seemed as though it would never end, of tall and beautiful women armed and equipped for war. They carried bows, and the children noticed that one side of their chests was flatter than the other. And the procession went on and on, passing along the bridge and through the golden gate, till Cathay grew quite dizzy; and at last Mavis said, "Oh, your Majesty, do stop them. I'm sure there are heaps, and we shall be too late if we wait for any more."

So the Queen stopped the procession and they went back to the Palace, where the Queen of the Amazons greeted Joan of Arc and the other ladies as though they were old acquaintances.

In a few moments their plans were laid. I wish I could describe to you the great fight between the Nice Book People and the others. But I have not time, and besides, the children did not see all of it, so I don't see why *you* should. It was fought out in the Palace gardens. The armies were fairly evenly matched as to numbers, because the Bookworms had let out a great many Barbarians, and these, though not so unpleasant as Mr. Murdstone and Mrs. Fairchild, were quite bad enough. The children were not allowed to join in the battle, which they would dearly have liked to do. Only from a safe distance they heard the sound of steel on steel, the whir of arrows, and the war cries of the combatants. And presently a stream of fugitives darkened the pearly pathways, and one could see the heroes with drawn swords following in pursuit.

And then, among those who were left, the shouts of war turned suddenly to shouts of laughter, and the Merlish Queen herself moved toward the battlefield. And as she drew near she, too, laughed. For, it would seem, the Amazons had only shot their arrows at the men among their foes — they had disdained to shoot the women, and so good was their aim that not a single woman was wounded. Only when the Book Hatefuls had been driven back by the Book Heroes, the Book Heroines advanced and, without more ado, fell on the remaining foes. They did not fight them with swords or spears or arrows or the short, sharp knives they wore — they simply picked up the screaming Bookwomen and carried them back to the books where they belonged. Each Amazon caught up one of the foe and, disregarding her screaming and scratching, carried her back to the book where she belonged, pushed her in, and shut the door.

Boadicea carried Mrs. Markham and her brown silk under one bare, braceleted arm as though she had been a naughty child. Joan of Arc made herself responsible for Aunt Fortune, and the Queen of the Amazons made nothing of picking up Miss Murdstone, beads and all, and carrying her in her arms like a baby. Torfrida's was the hardest task. She had, from the beginning, singled out Alftruda, her old and bitter enemy, and the fight between them was a fierce one, though it was but a battle of looks. Yet before long the fire in Torfrida's great dark eyes seemed to scorch her adversary, she shrank before it, and shrank and shrank till at last she turned and crept back to her book and went in of her own accord, and Torfrida shut the door.

"But" said Mavis, who had followed her, "don't you live in the same book?"

Torfrida smiled.

"Not quite," she said. "That would be impossible. I live in a different edition, where only the Nice People are alive. In hers it is the nasty ones."

"And where is Hereward ?" Cathay asked, before Mavis could stop her. "I do love him, don't you?"

"Yes," said Torfrida, "I love him. But he is not alive in the book where I live. But he will be — he will be."

And smiling and sighing, she opened her book and went into it, and the children went slowly back to the Palace. The fight was over, the Book People had gone back into their books, and it was almost as though they had never left them — not quite, for the children had seen the faces of the heroes, and the books where these lived could never again now be the same to them. All books, indeed, would now have an interest far above any they had ever held before — for any of these people might be found in any book. You never know.

The Princess Freia met them in the Palace courtyard, and clasped their hands and called them the preservers of the country, which was extremely pleasant. She also told them that a slight skirmish had been fought on the Mussel-beds south of the city, and the foe had retreated.

"But Reuben tells me," she added — "that boy is really worth his weight in pearls — that the main body are to attack at midnight. We must sleep now, to be ready for the call of duty when it comes. Sure you understand your duties? And the power of your buttons and your antidotes? I might not have time to remind you later. You can sleep in the armory — you must be awfully tired. You'll be asleep before you can say Jack Sprat."

So they lay down on the seaweed, heaped along one end of the Oysters' armory, and were instantly asleep.

BOOK HEROINES.

It may have been their natures, or it may have been the influence of the magic coats. But whatever the cause, it is certain that they lay down without fear, slept without dreams, and awoke without alarm when an Oyster corporal touched their arms and whispered, "Now!"

They were wide awake on the instant and started up, picking their oyster shields from the ground beside them.

"I feel just like a Roman soldier," Cathay said. "Don't you?"

And the others owned that so far as they knew the feelings of a Roman soldier, those feelings were their own.

The shadows of the guardroom were changed and shifted and flung here and there by the torches carried by the busy Oysters. Phosphorescent fish these torches were, and gave out a moony light like that of the pillars in the Cave of Learning. Outside the Lobster-guarded arch the water showed darkly clear. Large phosphorescent fish were twined round pillars of stone, rather like the fish you see on the lampposts on the Thames Embankment, only in this case the fish were the lamps. So strong was the illumination that you could see as clearly as you can on a moonlit night on the downs, where there are no trees to steal the light from the landscape and bury it in their thick branches.

All was hurry and bustle. The Salmoners had sent a detachment to harass the flank of the enemy, and the Sea Urchins, under the command of Reuben, were ready in their seaweed disguises.

There was a waiting time, and the children used it to practice with their shells, using the thick stems of seaweed — thick as a man's arm — to represent the ankles of the invading force, and they were soon fairly expert at the trick which was their duty. Francis had just nipped an extra fat stalk and released it again by touching the secret spring when the word went around, "Every man to his post!"

The children proudly took up their post next to the Princess, and hardly had they done so when a faint yet growing sound knocked gently at their ears. It grew and grew and grew till it seemed to shake the ground on which they stood, and the Princess murmured, "It is the tramp of the army of the Under Folk. Now, be ready. We shall lurk among these rocks. Hold your good oyster shell in readiness, and when you see a foot near you clip it, and at the same time set down the base of the shell on the rock. The trusty shell will do the rest."

"Yes, we know, thank you, dear Princess," said Mavis. "Didn't you see us practicing?"

But the Princess was not listening; she had enough to do to find cover for her troops among the limpet-studded rocks.

And now the tramp, tramp, tramp of the great army sounded nearer and more near, and through the dimly lighted water the children could see the great Deep Sea People advancing.

Very terrible they were, big beyond man-size, more stalwart and more finely knit than the Forlorn Hopers who had led the attack so happily and gloriously frustrated by the Crabs, the Narwhals and the Sea Urchins. As the advance guard drew near all the children stared, from their places of concealment, at the faces of these terrible foes of the happy Merland. Very strong the faces were, and, surprisingly, very, very sad. They looked — Francis at least was able to see it — like strong folk suffering proudly an almost intolerable injury — bearing, bravely, an almost intolerable pain.

"But I'm on the other side," he told himself, to check a sudden rising in his heart of — well, if it was not sympathy, what was it?

And now the head of the advancing column was level with the Princess. True to the old tradition which bids a commander lead and not to follow his troops, she was the first to dart out and fix a shell to the heel of the left-rank man. The children were next. Their practice bore its fruit. There was no blunder, no mistake. Each oyster shell clipped sharp and clean the attached ankle of an enemy; each oyster shell at the same moment attached itself firmly to the rock, thus clinging to his base in the most thorough and military way. A spring of joy and triumph welled up in the children's hearts. How easy it was to get the better of these foolish Deep Sea Folk. A faint, kindly contempt floated into the children's minds for the Mer-people, who so dreaded and hated these stupid giants. Why, there were fifty or sixty of them tied by the leg already! It was as easy as —

The pleasant nature of these reflections had kept our four rooted to the spot. In the triumphant performance of one duty they failed to remember the duty that should have followed. They stood there rejoicing in their victory, when by all the rules of the Service they should have rushed back to the armory for fresh weapons.

The omission was fatal. Even as they stood there rejoicing in their cleverness and boldness and in the helpless anger of the enemy, something thin and string-like spread itself around them — their feet caught in string, their fingers caught in string, string tweaked their ears and flattened their noses — string confined their elbows and confused their legs. The Lobster-guarded doorway seemed farther off — and farther, and farther... They turned their heads; they were following backward, and against their will, a retreating enemy.

"Oh, why didn't we do what she said?" breathed Cathay. "Something's happened!"

"I should think it had," said Bernard. "We're caught — in a net."

They were. And a tall Infantryman of the Under Folk was towing them away from Merland as swiftly and as easily as a running child tows a captive air balloon.

The Under Folk

Those of us who have had the misfortune to be caught in a net in the execution of our military duty, and to be dragged away by the enemy with all the helpless buoyancy of captive balloons, will be able to appreciate the sensations of the four children to whom this gloomy catastrophe had occurred.

The net was very strong — made of twisted fibrous filaments of seaweed. All efforts to break it were vain, and they had, unfortunately, nothing to cut it with. They had not even their oyster shells, the rough edges of which might have done something to help, or at least would have been useful weapons, and the discomfort of their position was extreme. They were, as Cathay put it, "all mixed up with each other's arms and legs," and it was very difficult and painful to sort themselves out without hurting each other.

"Let's do it, one at a time," said Mavis, after some minutes of severe and unsuccessful struggle. "France first. Get right away, France, and see if you can't sit down on a piece of the net that isn't covered with *us*, and then Cathay can try."

It was excellent advice and when all four had followed it, it was found possible to sit side by side on what may be called the floor of the net, only the squeezing of the net walls tended to jerk one up from one's place if one wasn't very careful.

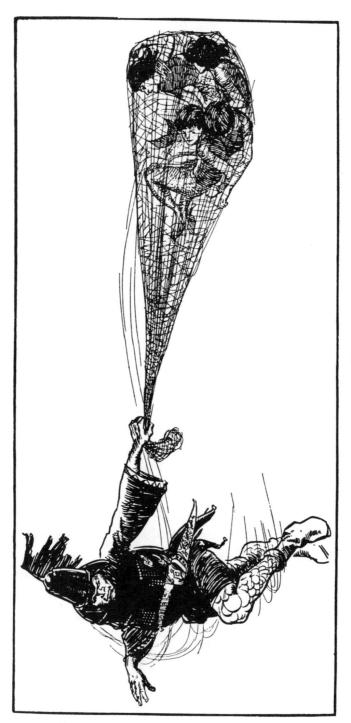

In the Net.

By the time the rearrangement was complete, and they were free to look about them, the whole aspect of the world had changed. The world, for one thing, was much darker, in itself that is, though the part of it where the children were was much lighter than had been the sea where they were first netted. It was a curious scene — rather like looking down on London at night from the top of St. Paul's. Some bright things, like trams or omnibuses, were rushing along, and smaller lights, which looked mighty like cabs and carriages, dotted the expanse of blackness till, where they were thick set, the darkness disappeared in a blaze of silvery light.

Other light-bearers had rows of round lights like the portholes of great liners. One came sweeping toward them, and a wild idea came to Cathay that perhaps when ships sink they go on living and moving underwater just as she and the others had done. Perhaps they do. Anyhow, this was not one of them, for, as it came close, it was plainly to be perceived as a vast fish with phosphorescent lights in rows along its gigantic sides. It opened its jaws as it passed, and for an instant everyone shut their eyes and felt that all was over. When the eyes were again, the mighty fish was far away. Cathay, however, was discovered to be in tears.

"I wish we hadn't come," she said; and the others could not but feel that there was something in what she said. They comforted her and themselves as best they could by expressing a curious half-certainty which they had that everything would be all right in the end. As I said before, there are some things so horrible that if you can bring yourself to face them you see at once that they can't be true. The barest idea of poetic justice — which we all believe in at the bottom of our hearts — made it impossible to think that the children who had nobly (they couldn't help feeling it *was* noble) defended their friends, the Mer Folk, should have anything really dreadful happen to them in consequence. And when Bernard talked about the fortunes of war he did it in an unconvinced sort of way and Francis told him to shut up.

"But what are we to do," sniffed Cathay for the twentieth time, and all the while the Infantryman was going steadily on, dragging the wretched netful after him.

"Press our pearl buttons," suggested Francis hopefully. "Then we shall be invisible and unfeelable and we can escape." He fumbled with the round marblelike pearl.

"No, no," said Bernard, catching at his hand, "don't you see? If we do, we may never get out of the net. If they can't see us or feel us they'll think the net's empty, and perhaps hang it up on a hook or put it away in a box."

"And forget it while years roll by. I see," said Cathay.

"But we can undo them the minute we're there. Can't we?" said Mavis.

"Yes, of course," said Bernard; but as a matter of fact they couldn't.

At last the Infantryman, after threading his way through streets of enormous rocky palaces, passed through a colossal arch, and so into a hall as big as St. Paul's and Westminster Abbey into one.

A crowd of Under Folk, who were seated on stone benches around rude tables, eating strange luminous food, rose up, and cried, "What news?"

"Four prisoners," said the Infantryman.

"Upper Folk," the Colonel said; "and my orders are to deliver them to the Queen herself."

He passed to the end of the hall and up a long wide flight of steps made of something so green and clear that it was plainly either glass or emerald, and I don't think it could have been glass, because how could they have made glass in the sea? There were lights below it which shone through the green transparency so clear and lovely that Francis said dreamily —

"Sabrina fair
   Listen where thou art sitting
Under the glassie, cool, translucent wave,"

and quite suddenly there was much less room in the net, and they were being embraced all at once and with tears of relief and joy by the Princess Freia — their own Mer Princess.

"Oh, I *didn't* mean to — Princess dear, I *didn't*," said Francis. "It was the emerald steps made me think of trunslucent."

"So they are," she said, "but oh, if you knew what I've felt — you, our guests, our knight-errants, our noble defenders — to be prisoners and all of us safe. I did so *hope* you'd call me. And I'm so proud that you didn't — that you were brave enough not to call for me until you did it by accident."

"We never thought of doing it," said Mavis candidly, "but I hope we shouldn't have, if we *had* thought of it."

"Why haven't you pressed your pearl buttons?" she asked, and they told her why.

"Wise children," she said, "but at any rate we must all use the charm that prevents our losing our memories."

"I shan't use mine," said Cathay. "I don't want to remember. If I didn't remember I should forget to be frightened. Do please let me forget to remember." She clung pleadingly to the Princess, who whispered to Mavis, "Perhaps it would be best," and they let Cathay have her way.

The others had only just time to swallow their charms before the Infantryman threw the net on to a great table, which seemed to be cut out of one vast diamond, and fell on his face on the ground. It was his way of saluting his sovereign.

"Prisoners, your Majesty," he said when he had got up again. "Four of the young of the Upper Folk — and he turned to the net as he spoke, and stopped short — "there's someone else," he said in an altered voice, "someone as wasn't there when we started, I'll swear."

"Open the net," said a strong, sweet voice, "and bid the prisoners stand up that I may look upon them."

"They might escape, my love," said another voice anxiously, "or perhaps they bite."

"Submersia," said the first voice, "do you and four of my women stand ready. Take the prisoners one by one. Seize each a prisoner and hold them, awaiting my royal pleasure."

The net was opened and large and strong hands took Bernard, who was nearest the mouth of the net back, and held him gently but with extreme firmness in an upright position on the table. None of them could stand because of their tails.

They saw before them, on a throne, a tall and splendid Queen, very beautiful and very sad, and by her side a King (they knew the royalty by their crowns), not so handsome as his wife, but still very different from the uncouth, heavy Under Folk. And he looked sad too. They were clad in robes of richest woven seaweed, sewn with jewels, and their crowns were like dreams of magnificence. Their throne was of one clear blood-bright ruby, and its canopy of green drooping seaweed was gemmed with topazes and amethysts. The Queen rose and came down the steps of the throne and whispered to her whom she had called Submersia, and she in turn whispered to the four other large ladies who held, each, a captive.

And with a dreadful unanimity the five acted; with one dexterous movement they took off the magic jackets, and with another they removed the useful tails. The Princess and the four children stood upon the table on their own ten feet.

"What funny little things," said the King, not unkindly.

"Hush," said the Queen, "perhaps they can understand what you say — and at any rate that Mer-girl can."

The children were furious to hear their Princess so disrespectfully spoken of. But she herself remained beautifully calm.

"Now," said the Queen, "before we destroy your memories, will you answer questions?"

"Some questions, yes — others, no," said the Princess.

"Are these human children?"

"Yes."

"How do they come under the sea?"

"Mer-magic. You wouldn't understand," said the Princess haughtily.

"Were they fighting against us?"

"Yes," cried Bernard and Mavis before the Princess answered.

"And lucky to do it," Francis added.

"If you will tell us the fighting strength of the Merlanders, your tails and coats shall be restored to you and you shall go free. Will you tell?"

"Is it likely?" the Princess answered. "I am a Mer-woman, and a Princess of the Royal House. Such do not betray their country."

"No, I suppose not," said the Queen. And she paused a moment before she said, "Administer the cup of forgetfulness."

The cup of forgetfulness was exceedingly pleasant. It tasted of toffee and coconuts, and pineapple ices, and plum cake, and roast chicken, with a faint underflavor of lavender, rose leaves and the very best *eau de cologne*.

The children had tasted cider-cup and champagne-cup at parties, and had disliked both, but oblivion-cup was delicious. It was served in a goblet of opal color, in dreamy pink and pearl — and green and blue and gray — and the sides of the goblet were engraved with pictures of beautiful people asleep. The goblet passed from hand to hand, and when each had drunk enough the Lord High Cupbearer, a very handsome, reserved-looking fish, laid a restraining touch on the goblet and, taking it between his fins, handed it to the next drinker. So, one by one, each took the draught. Kathleen was the last.

The draught had no effect on four out of the five — but Kathleen changed before their eyes, and though they had known that the draught of oblivion would make her forget, it was terrible to see it do its fell work.

Mavis had her arm protectingly around Kathleen, and the moment the draught had been swallowed Kathleen threw off that loving arm and drew herself away. It hurt like a knife. Then she looked at her brothers and sisters, and it is a very terrible thing when the eyes you love look at you as though you were a stranger.

Now, it had been agreed, while still the captives were in the net, that all of them should pretend that the cup of oblivion had taken effect, that they should just keep still and say nothing and look as stupid as they could. But this coldness of her dear Cathay's was more than Mavis could bear, and no one had counted on it. So when Cathay looked at Mavis as at a stranger whom she rather disliked, and drew away from her arm, Mavis could not bear it, and cried out in heart-piercing tones, "Oh, Cathay, darling, what is it? What's the matter?" before the Princess or the boys could stop her. And to make matters worse, both boys said in a very loud, plain whisper, "Shut up, Mavis," and only the Princess kept enough presence of mind to go on saying nothing.

Cathay turned and looked at her sister.

"Cathay, darling," Mavis said again, and stopped, for no one could go on saying "darling" to anyone who looked at you as Cathay was looking.

She turned her eyes away as Cathay looked toward the Queen — looked, and went, to lean against the royal knee as though it had been her mother's.

"Dear little thing," said the Queen; "see, it's quite tame. I shall keep it for a pet. Nice little pet then!"

"You shan't keep her," cried Mavis, but again the Princess hushed her, and the Queen treated her cry with contemptuous indifference. Cathay snuggled against her new mistress.

"As for the rest of you," said the Queen, "it is evident from your manner that the draught of oblivion has not yet taken effect on you. So it is impossible for me to make presents of you to those prominent members of the nobility, who are wanting pets, as I should otherwise have done. We will try another draught tomorrow. In the meantime... the fetters, Jailer."

A tall sour-looking Under-man stepped forward. Hanging over his arm were scaly tails, which at first sight of the children's hearts leaped, for they hoped they were their own. But no sooner were the tails fitted on than they knew the bitter truth.

"Yes," said the Queen "they are false tails. You will not be able to take them off, and you can neither swim nor walk with them. You can, however, move along quite comfortably on the floor of the ocean. What's the matter?" she asked the Jailer.

"None of the tails will fit this prisoner, your Majesty," said the Jailer.

"I am a Princess of the reigning Mer House," said Freia, "and your false, degrading tails cannot cling to me."

"Oh, put them all in the lockup," said the King, "as sullen a lot of prisoners as ever I saw — what?"

The lockup was a great building, broader at the top than at the bottom, which seemed to be balanced on the sea floor, but really it was propped up at both ends with great chunks of rock. The prisoners were taken there in the net, and being dragged along in nets is so confusing, that it was not till the Jailer had left them that they discovered that the prison was really a ship — an enormous ship — which lay there, perfect in every detail

as on the day when it first left dock. The water did not seem to
have spoiled it at all. They were imprisoned in the saloon, and,
worn out with the varied emotions of the day, they lay down on
the comfortable red velvet cushions and went to sleep. Even
Mavis felt that Kathleen had found a friend in the Queen, and
was in no danger.

The Princess was the last to close her eyes. She looked long
at the sleeping children.

"Oh, *why* don't they think of it?" she said, "and why mustn't
I tell them?"

There was no answer to either question, and presently she
too slept.

I must own that I share the Princess's wonder that the
children did not spend the night in saying "Sabrina fair" over
and over again. Because, of course, each invocation would have
been answered by an inhabitant of Merland, and thus a small
army could easily have been collected, the Jailer overpowered
and a rush made for freedom.

I wish I had time to tell you all that happened to Kathleen,
because the daily life of a pampered lap-child to a reigning
Queen is one that you would find most interesting to read about.
As interesting as your Rover or Binkie would find it to read —
if he could read — about the life of one of Queen Alexandra's
Japanese Spaniels. But time is getting on, and I must make a
long story short. And anyhow you can never tell all about
everything, can you?

The next day the Jailers brought food to the prison, as well
as a second draught of oblivion, which, of course, had no effect,
and they spent the day wondering how they could escape. In the
evening the Jailer's son brought more food and more oblivion-
cup, and he lingered while they ate. He did not look at all
unkind, and Francis ventured to speak to him.

"I say," he said.

"What do you say?" the Under-lad asked.

"Are you forbidden to talk to us?"

"No."

"Then do tell us what they will do with us."

"I do not know. But we shall have to know before long. The prisons are filling up quickly — they will soon be quite full. Then we shall have to let some of you out on what is called ticket-of-leave — that means with your artificial tails on, which prevent you getting away, even if the oblivion-cup doesn't take effect."

"I say," Bernard's turn to ask.

"What do you say?"

"Why don't the King and Queen go and fight, like the Mer Royal Family do?"

"Against the law," said the Under-lad. "We took a King prisoner once, and our people were afraid our King and Queen might be taken, so they made that rule."

"What did you do with him — the prisoner King?" the Princess asked.

"Put him in an Iswater," said the lad, "a piece of water entirely surrounded by land."

"I should like to see him," said the Princess.

"Nothing easier," said the Mer-lad, "as soon as you get your tickets-of-leaves. It's a good long passage to the lake — nearly all water, of course, but lots of our young people go there three times a week. Of course, he can't be a King any more now — but they made him Professor of Conchology."

"And has he forgotten he was a *King*?" asked the Princess.

"Of course, but he was so learned the oblivion-cup wasn't deep enough to make him forget everything: that's why he's a Professor."

"What was he King of?" the Princess asked anxiously.

"He was King of the Barbarians," said the Jailer's son — and the Princess sighed.

"I thought it might have been my father," she said, "he was lost at sea, you know."

The Under-lad nodded sympathetically and went away.

"He doesn't seem such a bad sort," said Mavis.

"No," said the Princess, "I can't understand it. I thought all the Under Folk were terrible fierce creatures, cruel and implacable."

"And they don't seem so very different from us — except to look at," said Bernard.

"I wonder," said Mavis, "what the war began about?"

"Oh — we've always been enemies," said the Princess, carelessly.

"Yes — but how did you begin being enemies?"

"Oh, that," said the Princess, "is lost in the mists of antiquity, before the dawn of history and all that."

"Oh," said Mavis.

But when Ulfin came with the next meal — did I tell you that the Jailer's son's name was Ulfin? — Mavis asked him the same question.

"I don't know — little land-lady," said Ulfin, "but I will find out — my uncle is the Keeper of the National Archives, graven on tables of stone, so many that no one can count them, but there are smaller tables telling what is on the big ones — " he hesitated. "If I could get leave to show you the Hall of the Archives, would you promise not to try to escape?"

They had now been shut up for two days and would have promised anything in reason.

"You see, the prisons are quite full now," he said, "and I don't see why you shouldn't be the first to get your leaves-tickets. I'll ask my father."

"I say!" said Mavis.

"What do you say?" said Ulfin.

"Do you know anything about my sister?"

"The Queen's new lap-child? Oh — she's a great pet — her gold collar with her name on it came home today. My cousin's brother-in-law made it."

"The name — Kathleen?" said Mavis.

"The name on the collar is Fido," said Ulfin.

The next day Ulfin brought their tickets-of-leaves, made of the leaves of the tree of Liberty which grows at the bottom of the well where Truth lies.

"Don't lose them," he said, "and come with me." They found it quite possible to move along slowly on hands and tails, though they looked rather like seals as they did so.

He led them through the strange streets of massive passages, pointing out the buildings, giving them their names as you might do if you were showing the marvels of your own city to a stranger.

"That's the Astrologers' Tower," he said, pointing to a huge building high above the others. "The wise men sit there and observe the stars."

"But you can't see the stars down here."

"Oh, yes, we can. The tower is fitted up with tubes and mirrors and water transparence apparatus. The wisest men in the country are there — all but the Professor of Conchology. He's the wisest of all. He invented the nets that caught you — or rather, making nets was one of the things that he had learned and couldn't forget."

"But who thought of using them for catching prisoners?"

"I did," said Ulfin proudly, "I'm to have a glass medal for it."

"Do you have glass down here?"

"A little comes down, you know. It is very precious. We engrave it. That is the Library — millions of tables of stone — the Hall of Public Joy is next to it — that garden is the mothers' garden where they go to rest while their children are at school — that's one of our schools. And here's the Hall of Public Archives."

THE HALL OF PUBLIC ARCHIVES.

The Keeper of the Records received them with grave courtesy. The daily services of Ulfin had accustomed the children to the appearance of the Under Folk, and they no longer found their strange, mournful faces terrifying, and the great hall where, on shelves cut out of the sheer rock, were stored the graven tables of Underworld Records, was very wonderful and impressive.

"What is it you want to know?" said the Keeper, rolling away some of the stones he had been showing them. "Ulfin said there was something special."

"Why the war began?" said Francis.

"Why the King and Queen are different?" said Mavis.

"The war," said the Keeper of the Records, "began exactly three million five hundred and seventy-nine thousand three hundred and eight years ago. An Under-man, getting off his Sea Horse in a hurry trod on the tail of a sleeping Merman. He did not apologize because he was under a vow not to speak for a year and a day. If the Mer-people had only waited he would have explained, but they went to war at once, and, of course, after that you couldn't expect him to apologize. And the war has gone on, off and on and on and off, ever since."

"And won't it ever stop?" asked Bernard.

"Not till *we* apologize, which, of course, we can't until *they* find out why the war began and that it wasn't our fault."

"How awful!" said Mavis; "then it's all really about nothing."

"Quite so," said the Keeper, "what are your wars about? The other question I shouldn't answer only I know you'll forget it when the oblivion-cup begins to work. Ulfin tells me it hasn't begun yet. Our King and Queen are *imported*. We used to be a Republic, but Presidents were so uppish and so grasping, and all their friends and relations too; so we decided to be a Monarchy, and that all jealousies might be taken away we imported the two handsomest Land Folk we could find. They've been a great success, and as they have no relations we find it much less expensive.

When the Keeper had thus kindly gratified the curiosity of the prisoners the Princess said suddenly:

"Couldn't *we* learn Conchology?"

And the Keeper said kindly, "Why not? It's the Professor's day tomorrow."

"Couldn't we go there today?" asked the Princess, "just to arrange about times and terms and all that?"

"If my Uncle says I may take you there," said Ulfin, "I will, for I have never known any pleasure so great as doing anything that you wish will give me."

The Uncle looked a little anxious, but he said he thought there could be no harm in calling on the Professor. So they went. The way was long for people who were not seals by nature and were not yet compelled to walk after the manner of those charming and intelligent animals. The Mer Princess alone was at her ease. But when they passed a building, as long as from here to the end of the Mile End Road, which Ulfin told them was the Cavalry Barracks, a young Under-man leaned out of a window and said:

"What ho! Ulf."

"What ho! yourself," said Ulfin, and approaching the window spoke in whispers. Two minutes later the young Cavalry Officer who had leaned out of the window gave an order, and almost at once some magnificent Sea Horses, richly caparisoned, came out from under an arched gateway. The three children were mounted on these, and the crowd which had collected in the street seemed to find it most amusing to see people in fetter-tails riding on the chargers of the Horse Marines. But their laughter was not ill-natured. And the horses were indeed a boon to the weary tails of the amateur seals.

THE CHARGERS OF THE HORSE MARINES.

Riding along the bottom of the sea was a wonderful experience — but soon the open country was left behind and they began to go up ways cut in the heart of the rock — ways long and steep, and lighted, as all that great Underworld was, with phosphorescent light.

When they had been traveling for some hours and the children were beginning to think that you could perhaps have too much even of such an excellent thing as Sea Horse exercise, the phosphorescent lights suddenly stopped, and yet the sea was not dark. There seemed to be a light ahead, and it got stronger and stronger as they advanced, and presently it streamed down on them from shallow water above their heads.

"We leave the Sea Horses here," said Ulfin, "they cannot live in the air. Come."

They dismounted and swam up. At least Ulfin and the Princess swam and the others held hands and were pulled by the two swimmers. Almost at once their heads struck the surface of the water, and there they were, on the verge of a rocky shore. They landed, and walked — if you can call what seals do walking — across a ridge of land, then plunged into a landlocked lake that lay beyond.

"This is the Iswater," said Ulfin as they touched bottom, "and yonder is the King." And indeed a stately figure in long robes was coming toward them.

"But this," said the Princess, trembling, "is just like our garden at home, only smaller."

"It was made as it is," said Ulfin, "by wish of the captive King. Majesty is Majesty, be it never so conquered."

The advancing figure was now quite near them. It saluted them with royal courtesy.

"We wanted to know," said Mavis, "please, your Majesty, if we might have lessons from you."

The King answered, but the Princess did not hear. She was speaking with Ulfin, apart.

"Ulfin," she said, "this captive King is my Father."

"Yes, Princess," said Ulfin.

"And he does not know me — "

"He will," said Ulfin strongly.

"Did you know?"

"Yes."

"But the people of your land will punish you for bringing us here, if they find out that he is my father and that you have brought us together. They will kill you. Why did you do it, Ulfin?"

"Because you wished it, Princess," he said, "and because I would rather die for you than live without you."

The Peacemaker

T he children thought they had never seen a kinder face or more noble bearing than that of the Professor of Conchology, but the Mer Princess could not bear to look at him. She now felt what Mavis had felt when Cathay failed to recognize her — the misery of being looked at without recognition by the eyes that we know and love. She turned away, and pretended to be looking at the leaves of the seaweed hedge while Mavis and Francis were arranging to take lessons in Conchology three days a week, from two to four.

"You had better join a class," said the Professor, "you will learn less that way."

"But we want to learn," said Mavis.

And the Professor looked at her very searchingly and said, "Do you?"

"Yes," she said, "at least — "

"Yes," he said, "I quite understand. I am only an exiled Professor, teaching Conchology to youthful aliens, but I retain some remnants of the wisdom of my many years. I know that I am not what I seem, and that you are not what you seem, and that your desire to learn my special subject is not sincere and wholehearted, but is merely, or mainly, the cloak to some other design. Is it not so, my child?"

No one answered. His question was so plainly addressed to the Princess. And she must have felt the question, for she turned and said, "Yes, O most wise King."

"I am no King," said the Professor, "rather I am a weak child picking up pebbles by the shore of an infinite sea of knowledge."

"You *are*," the Princess was beginning impulsively, when Ulfin interrupted her.

"Lady, lady!" he said, "all will be lost! Can you not play your part better than this? If you continue these indiscretions my head will undoubtedly pay the forfeit. Not that I should for a moment grudge that trifling service, but if my head is cut off you will be left without a friend in this strange country, and I shall die with the annoying consciousness that I shall no longer be able to serve you."

He whispered this into the Princess's ear while the Professor of Conchology looked on with mild surprise.

"Your attendant," he observed, "is eloquent but inaudible."

"I mean to be," said Ulfin, with a sudden change of manner. "Look here, sir, I don't suppose you care what becomes of you."

"Not in the least," said the Professor.

"But I suppose you would be sorry if anything uncomfortable happened to your new pupils?"

"Yes," said the Professor, and his eye dwelt on Freia.

"Then please concentrate your powerful mind on being a Professor. Think of nothing else. More depends on this than you can easily believe."

"Believing is easy," said the Professor. "Tomorrow at two, I think you said?" and with a grave salutation he turned his back on the company and walked away through his garden.

It was a thoughtful party that rode home on the borrowed chargers of the Deep Sea Cavalry. No one spoke. The minds of all were busy with the strange words of Ulfin, and even the least imaginative of them, which in this case was Bernard, could not but think that Ulfin had in that strange oddly shaped head of his, some plan for helping the prisoners, to one of whom at least he was so obviously attached. He also was silent, and the others could not help encouraging the hope that he was maturing plans.

They reached the many-windowed prison, gave up their tickets-of-leaves and reentered it. It was not till they were in the saloon and the evening was all but over that Bernard spoke of what was in every head.

"Look here," he said, "I think Ulfin means to help us to escape."

"Do you," said Mavis. "I think he means to help us to something, but I don't somehow think it's as simple as that."

"Nothing near," said Francis simply.

"But that's all we want, isn't it?" said Bernard.

"It's not all *I* want," said Mavis, finishing the last of a fine bunch of sea-grapes, "what I want is to get the Mer King restored to his sorrowing relations."

The Mer Princess pressed her hand affectionately.

"So do I," said Francis, "but I want something more than that even. I want to stop this war. For always. So that there'll never be any more of it."

"But how can you," said the Mer Princess, leaning her elbows on the table, "there's always been war; there always will be."

"Why?" asked Francis.

"I don't know; it's Merman nature, I suppose."

"I don't believe it," said Francis earnestly, "not for a minute I don't. Why, don't you see, all these people you're at war with are *nice*. Look how kind the Queen is to Cathay — look how kind Ulfin is to us — and the Librarian, and the Keeper of the Archives, and the soldiers who lent us the horses. They're all as decent as they can stick, and all the Mer-people are nice too — and then they all go killing each other, and all those brave, jolly soldier fish too, just all about nothing. I call it simply *rot*."

"But there always has been war I tell you," said the Mer Princess, "people would get slack and silly and cowardly if there were no wars."

"If I were King," said Francis, who was now thoroughly roused, "there should never be any more wars. There are plenty of things to be brave about without hurting other brave people — exploring and rescuing and saving your comrades in mines and in fires and floods and things and — " his eloquence suddenly gave way to a breathless shyness — "oh, well," he ended, "it's no use gassing; you know what I mean."

"Yes," said Mavis, "and oh, France — I think you're right. But what can we *do*?"

"I shall ask to see the Queen of the Under Folk, and try to make her see sense. She didn't look an absolute duffer."

They all gasped at the glorious and simple daring of the idea. But the Mer Princess said:

"I know you'd do everything you could — but it's very difficult to talk to kings unless you've been accustomed to it. There are books in the cave, *Straight Talks with Monarchs*, and *Kings I have Spoken my Mind To*, which might help you. But, unfortunately, we can't get them. You see, Kings start so much further than subjects do: they know such a lot more. Why, even I — "

"Then why won't *you* try talking to the Queen?"

"I shouldn't dare," said Freia. "I'm only a girl-Princess. Oh, if only my dear Father could talk to her. If he believed it possible that war could cease... *he* could persuade anybody of anything. And, of course, they would start on the same footing — both Monarchs, you know."

"I see: like belonging to the same club," said Francis vaguely.

"But, of course, as things are, my royal Father thinks of nothing but shells — if only we could restore his memory."

"I say," said Bernard suddenly, "does that Keep-your-Memory charm work backward?"

"Backward?"

"I mean — is it any use taking it after you've swallowed your dose of oblivion-cup? Is it a rester what's its name as well as an antidote?"

"Surely," said the Princess, "it is a restorative; only we have no charm to give my Father — they are not made in this country — and alas! we cannot escape and go to our own kingdom and return with one."

"No need," said Bernard, with growing excitement, "no need. Cathay's charm is there, in the inner pocket of her magic coat. If we could get that, give the charm to your Father, and then get him an interview with the Queen?"

"But what about Cathay?" said Mavis.

"If my Father's memory were restored," said the Princess, "his wisdom would find us a way out of all our difficulties. To find Cathay's coat: that is what we have to do."

"Yes," said Francis. "That's all." He spoke a little bitterly, for he had really rather looked forward to that straight talk with the King, and the others had not been as enthusiastic as he felt he had a right to expect.

"Let's call Ulfin," said the Princess, and they all scratched on the door of polished bird's-eye maple which separated their apartments from the rest of the prison. The electric bells were out of order, so one scratched instead of ringing. It was quite as easy.

Ulfin came with all speed.

"We're holding a council," said Freia, "and we want you to help. We know you will."

"I know it," said Ulfin, "tell me your needs — "

And without more ado they told him all.

"You trust me, Princess, I am proud," he told her, but when he heard Francis's dream of universal peace he took the freckled paw of Francis and laid his lips to it. And Francis, even in the midst of his pride and embarrassment at this token, could not help noticing that the lips of Ulfin were hard, like horn.

"I kiss your hand," said Ulfin, "because you give me back my honor, which I was willing to lay down, with all else, for the Princess to walk on to safety and escape. I would have helped you to find the hidden coat — for her sake alone, and that would have been a sin against my honor and my country — but now that I know it is to lead to peace, which, warriors as we are, the whole nation passionately desires, then I am acting as a true and honorable patriot. My only regret is that I have one gift the less to lay at the feet of the Princess."

"Do you know where the coats are?" Mavis asked.

"They are in the Foreign Curiosities Museum," said Ulfin, "strongly guarded: but the guards are the Horse Marines — whose officer lent you your chargers today. He is my friend, and when I tell him what is toward, he will help me. I only ask of you one promise in return. That you will not seek to escape, or to return to your own country, except by the free leave and license of our gracious Sovereigns."

The children easily promised — and they thought the promise would be easily kept.

"Then tomorrow," said Ulfin, "shall begin the splendid Peace Plot which shall hand our names down, haloed with glory, to remotest ages."

He looked kindly on them and went out.

"He *is* a dear, isn't he?" said Mavis.

"Yes, indeed," said the Princess absently.

And now next day the children, carrying their tickets-of-leaves, were led to the great pearl and turquoise building, which was the Museum of Foreign Curiosities. Many were the strange objects preserved there — china and glass and books and land — things of all kinds, taken from sunken ships. And all the things were under dome-shaped cases, apparently of glass. The

Curator of the Museum showed them his treasures with pride, and explained them all wrong in the most interesting way.

"Those discs," he said, pointing to the china plates, "are used in games of skill. They are thrown from one hand to another, and if one fails to catch them his head is broken."

An egg boiler, he explained, was a Land Queen's jewel case, and four egg-shaped emeralds had been fitted into it to show its use to the vulgar. A silver ice pail was labeled: "Drinking Vessel of the Horses of the Kings of Earth," and a cigar case half full was called "Charm case containing Evil Charms: probably Ancient Barbarian." In fact it was very like the museums you see on land.

They were just coming to a large case containing something whitish and labeled, "Very valuable indeed," when a messenger came to tell the Curator that a soldier was waiting with valuable curiosities taken as loot from the enemy.

"Excuse me one moment," said the Curator, and left them.

"*I* arranged that," said Ulfin, "quick, before he returns — take your coats if you know any spell to remove the case."

The Princess laughed and laid her hand on the glassy dome, and lo! it broke and disappeared as a bubble does when you touch it.

"Magic," whispered Ulfin.

"Not magic," said the Princess. "Your cases are only bubbles."

"And I never knew," said Ulfin.

"No," said the Princess, "because you never dared to touch them."

The children were already busy pulling the coats off the ruby slab where they lay. "Here's Cathay's," whispered Mavis.

The Princess snatched it and her own pearly coat which, in one quick movement, she put on and buttoned over Cathay's little folded coat, holding this against her. "Quick," she said, "put yours on, all of you. Take your mer-tails on your arms.

They did. The soldiers at the end of the long hall had noticed the movements and came charging up toward them.

"Quick, quick!" said the Princess, "now — altogether. One, two, three. Press your third buttons."

The children did, and the soldiers tearing up the hall to arrest the breakers of the cases of the Museum — for by this time they could see what had happened — almost fell over each other in their confusion. For there, where a moment ago had been four children with fin-tail fetters, was now empty space, and beside the rifled Museum case stood only Ulfin.

And then an odd thing happened. Out of nowhere, as it seemed, a little pearly coat appeared, hanging alone in air (water, of course, it was really. Or was it?) It seemed to grow and to twine itself round Ulfin.

"Put it on," said a voice from invisibility, "put it on," and Ulfin did put it on.

The soldiers were close upon him. "Press the third button," cried the Princess, and Ulfin did so. But as his right hand sought the button, the foremost soldier caught his left arm with the bitter cry —

"Traitor, I arrest you in the King's name," and though he could now not see that he was holding anything, he could feel that he was, and he held on.

"The last button, Ulfin," cried the voice of the unseen Princess, "press the last button," and next moment the soldier, breathless with amazement and terror, was looking stupidly at his empty hand. Ulfin, as well as the three children and the Princess, was not only invisible but intangible, the soldiers could not see or feel anything.

And what is more, neither could the Princess or the children or Ulfin.

"Oh, where are you? Where am I?" cried Mavis.

"Silence," said the Princess, "we must keep together by our

voices, but that is dangerous. *A la porte!*" she added. How fortunate it was that none of the soldiers understood French!

As the five were invisible and intangible and as the soldiers were neither, it was easy to avoid them and to get to the arched doorway. The Princess got there first. There was no enemy near — all the soldiers were crowding around the rifled Museum case, talking and wondering, the soldier who had seized Ulfin explaining again and again how he had had the caitiff by the arm, "as solid as solid, and then, all in a minute, there was nothing — nothing at all," and his comrades trying their best to believe him. The Princess just waited, saying, "Are you there?" every three seconds, as though she had been at the telephone.

"Are you there?" said the Princess for the twenty-seventh time. And then Ulfin said, "I am here, Princess."

"We must have connecting links," she said — "bits of seaweed would do. If you hold a piece of seaweed in your hand I will take hold of the other end of it. We cannot feel the touch of each other's hands, but we shall feel the seaweed, and you will know, by its being drawn tight that I have hold of the other end. Get some pieces for the children too. Good stout seaweed, such as you made the nets of with which you captured us."

"Ah, Princess," he said, "how can I regret that enough? And yet how can I regret it at all since it has brought you to me."

"Peace, foolish child," said the Princess, and Ulfin's heart leaped for joy because, when a Princess calls a grown-up man "child," it means that she likes him more than a little, or else, of course, she would not take such a liberty. "But the seaweed," she added — "there is no time to lose."

"I have some in my pocket," said Ulfin, blushing, only she could not see that. "They keep me busy making nets in my spare time — I always have some string in my pocket."

A piece of stringy seaweed suddenly became visible as Ulfin took it out of his invisible pocket, which, of course, had the property of making its contents invisible too, so long as they remained in it. It floated toward the Princess, who caught the end nearest to her and held it fast.

"Where are you?" said a small voice.

It was Mavis — and almost at once Francis and Bernard were there too. The seaweed chain was explained to them, and they each held fast to their ends of the seaweed links. So that when the soldiers, a little late in the day, owing to the careful management of Ulfin's friend, reached the front door, there was nothing to be seen but four bits of seaweed floating down the street, which, of course, was the sort of thing that nobody could possibly notice unless they *knew*.

The bits of seaweed went drifting to the Barracks, and no one noticed that they floated on to the stables and that invisible hands loosed the halters of five Sea Horses. The soldier who ought to have been looking after the horses was deeply engaged in a game of Animal Grab with a comrade. The cards were of narwhal ivory, very fine, indeed, and jeweled on every pip. The invisible hands saddled the Sea Horses and invisible forms sprang to the saddles, and urged the horses forward.

The unfortunate Animal Grabber was roused from his game by the sight of five retreating steeds — saddled and bridled indeed, but, as far as he could see, riderless, and long before other horses could be got out and saddled the fugitives were out of sight and pursuit was vain. Just as before they went across country to the rock cut and then swam up, holding by the linking seaweed.

Because it was Tuesday and nearly two o'clock, the Professor of Conchology was making ready to receive pupils, which he did in an arbor of coral of various shades of pink, surrounded by specimen shells of all the simpler species. He was alone in the garden, and as they neared him, the Princess, the three children and Ulfin touched the necessary buttons and became once more visible and tangible.

"Ha," said the Professor, but without surprise. "Magic. A very neat trick, my dears, and excellently done."

"You need not remove your jacket," he added to Ulfin, who was pulling off his pearly coat. "The mental exercises in which we propose to engage do not require gymnasium costume."

But Ulfin went on taking off his coat, and when it was off he handed it to the Princess, who at once felt in its inner pocket, pulled out a little golden case and held it toward the Professor. It has been well said that no charm on earth — I mean underwater — is strong enough to make one forget one's antidote. The moment the Professor's eye fell on the little golden case, he held out his hand for it, and the Princess gave it to him. He opened it, and without hesitation as without haste, swallowed the charm.

Next moment the Princess was clasped in his arms, and the moment after that, still clasped there, was beginning a hurried explanation; but he stopped her.

"I know, my child, I know," he said. "You have brought me the charm which gives back to me my memory and makes a King of Merland out of a Professor of Conchology. But why, oh why, did you not bring me my coat — my pearly coat?" said the King, "it was in the case with the others."

No one had thought of it, and everyone felt and looked exceedingly silly, and no one spoke till Ulfin said, holding out the coat which the Princess had given back to him — "You will have this coat, Majesty. I have no right to the magic garments of your country."

"But," said Francis, "you need the coat more than anybody. The King shall have mine — I shan't want it if you'll let me go and ask for an interview with the King of the Under Folk."

"No, have mine," said Mavis — and "have mine," said Bernard, and the Princess said, "Of course, my Father will have mine." So they all protested at once. But the King raised his hand, and there was silence, and they saw that he no longer looked only a noble and learned gentleman, but that he looked every inch a King.

"Silence," he said, "if anyone speaks with the King and Queen of this land it is fitting that it should be I. See, we will go out by the backdoor, so as to avoid the other pupils who will soon be arriving in their thousands, for my Conchology Course is very popular. And as we go, tell me who is this man of the Under Folk who seems to be one of you" — ("I am the Princess' servant," Ulfin put in) — "and why you desire to speak with the King of this land."

So they made great haste to go out by the back way so as not to meet the Conchology students, and cautiously crept up to their horses — and, of course, the biggest and best horse was given to the King to ride. But when he saw how awkwardly their false tails adapted themselves to the saddle he said, "My daughter, you can remove these fetters."

"How?" said she. "My shell knife won't cut them."

"Bite through the strings of them with your little sharp teeth," said the King, "nothing but Princess teeth is sharp enough to cut through them. No, my son — it is not degrading. A true Princess cannot be degraded by anything that is for the good of her subjects and her friends."

So the Mer Princess willingly bit through the strings of the false tails — and everybody put on his or her proper tail again, with great comfort and enjoyment — and they all swam toward the town.

And as they went they heard a great noise of shouting, and saw parties of Under Folk flying as if in fear.

"I must make haste," said the King, "and see to it that our Peace Conference be not too late," — so they hurried on.

And the noise grew louder and louder, and the crowds of flying Under Folk thicker and fleeter, and by and by Ulfin made them stand back under the arch of the Astrologers' Tower to see what it was from which they fled. And there, along the streets of the great city of the Under Folk, came the flash of swords and the swirl of banners and the army of the Mer Folk came along between the great buildings of their foes, and on their helmets was the light of victory, and at their head, proud and splendid, rode the Princess Maia and — Reuben.

"Oh — Reuben, Reuben! We're saved," called Mavis, and would have darted out, but Francis put his hand over her mouth.

"Stop!" he said, "don't you remember we promised not to escape without the Queen's permission? Quick, quick to the Palace, to make peace before our armies can attack it."

"You speak well," said the Mer King. And Ulfin said, "This is no time for ceremony. Quick, quick, I will take you in by the tradesmen's entrance." And, turning their backs on that splendid and victorious procession, they marched to the back entrance of the royal Palace.

The End

The Queen of the Under Folk sat with her husband on their second-best throne, which was much more comfortable than their State one, though not so handsome. Their sad faces were lighted up with pleasure as they watched the gambols of their new pet, Fido, a dear little earth-child, who was playing with a ball of soft pink seaweed, patting it, and tossing it and running after it as prettily as any kitten.

"Dear little Fido," said the Queen, "come here then," and Fido, who had once been Cathay, came willingly to lean against the Queen's knee and be stroked and petted.

"I have curious dreams sometimes," said the Queen to the King, "dreams so vivid that they are more like memories."

"Has it ever occurred to you," said the King, "that we have no memories of our childhood, of our youth — ?"

"I believe," said the Queen slowly, "that *we* have tasted in our time of the oblivion-cup. There is no one like us in this land. If we were born here, why can we not remember our parents who must have been like us? And dearest — the dream that comes to me most often is that we once had a child and lost it — and that it was a child like us — "

"Fido," said the King in a low voice, "is like us." And he too, stroked the head of Cathay, who had forgotten everything except that she was Fido and bore the Queen's name on her collar. "But if you remember that we had a child it cannot be true — if we drank of the oblivion-cup, that is, because, of course, that would make us forget everything."

"It could not make a mother forget her child," said the Queen, and with the word caught up Fido-which-was-Cathay and kissed her.

"Nice Queen," purred Cathay-which-was-Fido, "I do love you."

"I am sure we had a child once," said the Queen, hugging her, "and that we have been made to forget."

Even as she spoke the hangings of cloth of gold, pieced together from the spoil of lost galleons, rustled at the touch of someone outside. The Queen dried her eyes, which needed it, and said, "Come in."

The arras was lifted and a tall figure entered. "Bless my soul," said the King of the Under Folk, "it's the Professor of Conchology."

"No," said the figure, advancing, "it is the King of the Mer-people. My brother King, my sister Queen, I greet you."

"This is most irregular," said the King.

"Never mind, dear," said the Queen, "let us hear what his Majesty has to say."

"I say — Let there be peace between our people," said the Mer King. "For countless ages these wars have been waged, for countless ages your people and mine have suffered. Even the origin of the war is lost in the mists of antiquity. Now I come to you, I, your prisoner — I was given to drink of the cup of oblivion and forgot who I was and whence I came. Now a counter-charm has given me back mind and memory. I come in the name of my people. If we have wronged you, we ask your forgiveness. If you have wronged us, we freely forgive you. Say: Shall it be peace, and shall all the sons of the sea live as brothers in love and kindliness for evermore?"

"Really," said the King of the Under Folk, "I think it is not at all a bad idea — but in confidence, and between Monarchs, I may tell you, sir, that I suspect my mind is not what it was. You, sir, seem to possess a truly royal grasp of your subject. My mind is so imperfect that I dare not consult it. But my heart —"

"Your heart says Yes," said the Queen. "So does mine. But our troops are besieging your city," she said, "they will say that in asking for peace you were paying the tribute of the vanquished."

"My people will not think this of me," said the King of Merland, "nor would your people think it of you. Let us join hands in peace and the love of royal brethren."

"What a dreadful noise they are making outside," said the King, and indeed the noise of shouting and singing was now to be heard on every side of the Palace.

"If there was a balcony now where we could show ourselves," suggested the King of Merland.

"The very thing," said the Queen, catching up her pet Fido-which-was-Cathay in her arms and leading the way to the great curtained arch at the end of the hall. She drew back the swinging, sweeping hangings of woven seaweed and stepped forth on the balcony — the two Kings close behind her. But she stopped short and staggered back a little, so that her husband had to put an arm about her to support her, when her first glance showed her that the people who were shouting outside the Palace were not, as she had supposed, Under Folk in some unexpected though welcome transport of loyal enthusiasm, but ranks on ranks of the enemy, the hated Mer Folk, all splendid and menacing in the pomp and circumstance of glorious war.

"It is the enemy!" gasped the Queen.

"It is my people," said the Mer King. "It is a beautiful thing in you, dear Queen, that you agreed to peace, without terms, while you thought you were victorious, and not because the legions of the Mer Folk were thundering at your gates. May I speak for us?"

They signed assent. And the Mer King stepped forward full into view of the crowd in the street below.

"My people," he said in a voice loud, yet soft, and very, very beautiful. And at the words the Mer Folk below looked up and recognized their long-lost King, and a shout went up that you could have heard a mile away.

The King raised his hand for silence.

"My people," he said, "brave men of Merland — let there be peace, now and forever, between us and our brave foes. The King and Queen of this land agreed to make unconditional peace while they believed themselves to be victorious. If victory has for today been with us, let us at least be the equals of our foes in generosity as in valor."

Another shout rang out. And the King of the Under Folk stepped forward.

"My people," he said, and the Under Folk came quickly forward toward him at the sound of his voice. "There shall be peace. Let these who were your foes this morning be your guests tonight and your friends and brothers for evermore. If we have wronged them, we beg them to forgive us: if they have wronged us, we beg them to allow us to forgive them." ("Is that right?" he asked the Mer King in a hasty whisper, who whispered back, "Admirable!") "Now," he went on, "cheer, Mer Folk and Under Folk, for the splendid compact of Peace."

And they cheered.

"Pardon, your Majesty," — it was Ulfin who spoke, — "it was the stranger Francis who first conceived the Peace Idea."

"True," said the Mer King, "where *is* Francis?"

But Francis was not to be found; it was only his name which was presented to the people from the balcony. He himself kept his pearly coat on and kept the invisibility button well pressed down, till the crowd had dispersed to ring all the diving bells with which the towers of the city were so handsomely fitted up, to hang the city with a thousand seaweed flags, and to illuminate its every window and door and pinnacle and buttress with more and more phosphorescent fish. In the Palace was a banquet for the Kings and the Queen and the Princesses, and the three children, and Cathay-who-was-Fido. Also Reuben was called from the command of his Sea Urchins to be a guest at the royal table. Princess Freia asked that an invitation might be sent to Ulfin — but when the King's Private Secretary, a very intelligent cuttlefish, had got the invitation ready, handsomely written in his own ink, it was discovered that no Ulfin was to be found to receive it.

It was a glorious banquet. The only blot on its rapturous splendor was the fact that Cathay still remained Fido, the Queen's pet — and her eyes were still those cold, unremembering eyes which her brothers and sister could not bear to meet. Reuben sat at the right hand of the Queen, and from the moment he took his place there he seemed to think of no one else. He talked with her, sensibly and modestly, and Francis remarked that during his stay in Merland Reuben had learned to talk as you do, and not in the language of gypsy circus-people. The Commander-in-Chief of the Forces of the Under Folk sat at the left hand of his King. The King of the Mer Folk sat between his happy daughters, and the children sat together between the Chief Astrologer and the Curator of the Museum of Foreign Curiosities, who was more pleased to see them again than he had ever expected to be, and much more friendly than they had ever hoped to find him. Everyone was extremely happy, even Fido-which-was-Cathay, who sat on the Queen's lap and was fed with delicacies from the Queen's own plate.

It was at about the middle of the feast, just after everybody had drunk the health of the two Commanders-in-Chief, amid tempestuous applause, that a serving-fish whispered behind his fin to the Under Folk Queen:

"Certainly," she said, "show him in."

And the person who was shown in was Ulfin, and he carried on his arm a pearly coat and a scaly tail. He sank on one knee and held them up to the Mer King, with only one doubtful deprecating glance at the Curator of the Museum of Foreign Curiosities.

The King took them, and feeling in the pocket of the coat drew out three golden cases.

"It is the royal prerogative to have three," he said smilingly to the Queen, "in case of accidents. May I ask your Majesty's permission to administer one of them to your Majesty's little pet. I am sure you are longing to restore her to her brothers and her sister."

The Queen could not but agree — though her heart was sore at losing the little Fido-Kathleen, of whom she had grown so fond. But she was hoping that Reuben would consent to let her adopt him, and be more to her than many Fidos. She administered the charm herself, and the moment Cathay had swallowed it the royal arms were loosened, and the Queen expected her pet to fly to her brothers and sister. But to Cathay it was as though only an instant had passed since she came into that hall, a prisoner. So that when suddenly she saw her brothers and sister honored guests at what was unmistakably a very grand and happy festival, and found herself in the place of honor on the very lap of the Queen, she only snuggled closer to that royal lady and called out very loud and clear, "Hullo, Mavis! Here's a jolly transformation scene. That was a magic drink she gave us and it's made everybody jolly and friends —

I am glad. You dear Queen," she added, "it *is* nice of you to nurse me."

So everybody was pleased: only Princess Freia looked sad and puzzled and her eyes followed Ulfin as he bowed and made to retire from the royal presence. He had almost reached the door when she spoke quickly in the royal ear that was next to her.

"Oh, Father," she said, "don't let him go like that. He ought to be at the banquet. We couldn't have done anything without him."

"True," said the King, "but I thought he had been invited, and refused."

"Refused?" said the Princess, "oh, call him back!"

"I'll run if I may," said Mavis, slipping out of her place and running down the great hall.

"If you'll sit a little nearer to me, Father," said Maia obligingly, "the young man can sit between you and my sister."

So that is where Ulfin found himself, and that was where he had never dared to hope to be.

The banquet was a strange as well as a magnificent scene — because, of course, the Mer-people were beautiful as the day, the five children were quite as pretty as any five children have any need to be, and the King and Queen of the Under Folk were as handsome as handsome. So that all this handsomeness was a very curious contrast to the strange heavy features of the Under Folk who now sat at table, so pleasant and friendly, toasting their late enemies.

The contrast between the Princess Freia and Ulfin was particularly marked, for their heads bent near together as they talked.

"Princess," he was saying, "tomorrow you will go back to your kingdom, and I shall never see you again."

The Princess could not think of anything to say, because it seemed to her that what he said was true.

"But," he went on, "I shall be glad all my life to have known and loved so dear and beautiful a Princess."

And again the Princess could think of nothing to say.

"Princess," he said, "tell me one thing. Do you know what I should say to you if I were a Prince?"

"Yes," said Freia; "I know what you would say and I know what I should answer, dear Ulfin, if you were only a commoner of Merland... I mean, you know, if your face were like ours. But since you are of the Under Folk and I am a Mermaid, I can only say that I will never forget you, and that I will never marry anyone else."

"Is it only my face then that prevents your marrying me?" he asked with abrupt eagerness, and she answered gently, "Of course."

Then Ulfin sprang to his feet. "Your Majesties," he cried, "and Lord High Astrologer, has not the moment come when, since we are at a banquet with friends, we may unmask?"

The strangers exchanged wondering glances.

The Sovereigns and the Astrologers made gestures of assent — then, with a rustling and a rattling, helmets were unlaced and corselets unbuckled, the Under Folk seemed to the Mer-people as though they were taking off their very skins. But really what they took off was but their thick scaly armor, and under it they were as softly and richly clad, and as personable people as the Mer Folk themselves.

"But," said Maia — "how splendid! We thought you were always in armor — that — that it grew on you, you know."

The Under Folk laughed jollily. "Of course it was always on us — since — when you saw us, we were always at war."

"And you're just like us!" said Freia to Ulfin.

"There is no one like you," he whispered back. Ulfin was now a handsome dark-haired young man, and looked much more like a Prince than a great many real Princes do.

"Did you mean what you said just now?" the Princess whispered. And for answer Ulfin dared to touch her hand with soft firm fingers.

"Papa," said Freia, "please may I marry Ulfin?"

"By all means," said the King, and immediately announced the engagement, joining their hands and giving them his blessing in the most businesslike way.

Then said the Queen of the Under Folk:

"Why should not these two reign over the Under Folk and let us two be allowed to remember the things we have forgotten and go back to that other life which I know we had somewhere — where we had a child."

"I think," said Mavis, "that now everything's settled so comfortably we ought perhaps all of us to be thinking about getting home."

"I have only one charm left, unfortunately," said the Mer King, "but if your people will agree to your abdicating, I will divide it between you with pleasure, dear King and Queen of the Under Folk; and I have reason to believe that the half which you will each of you have, will be just enough to counteract your memories of this place, and restore to you all the memories of your other life."

"Could not Reuben go with us?" the Queen asked.

"No," said the Mer King, "but he shall follow you to earth, and that speedily."

The Astrologer Royal, who had been whispering to Reuben, here interposed.

"It would be well, your Majesties," he said, "if a small allowance of the cup of oblivion were served out to these land children, so that they may not remember their adventures here. It is not well for the Earth People to know too much of the dwellers in the sea. There is a sacred vessel which has long been preserved among the civic plate. I propose that this vessel should be presented to our guests as a mark of our esteem; that they shall bear it with them, and drink the contents as soon as they set foot on their own shores."

He was at once sent to fetch the sacred vessel. It was a stone ginger beer bottle.

"I do really think we ought to go," said Mavis again.

There were farewells to be said — a very loving farewell to the Princesses, a very friendly one to the fortunate Ulfin, and then a little party left the Palace quietly and for the last time made the journey to the quiet Iswater where the King of Merland had so long professed Conchology.

Arrived at this spot the King spoke to the King and Queen of the Under Folk.

"Swallow this charm," he said, "in equal shares — then rise to the surface of the lake and say the charm which I perceive the Earth children have taught you as we came along. The rest will be easy and beautiful. We shall never forget you, and your hearts will remember us, though your minds must forget. Farewell."

The King and Queen rose through the waters and disappeared.

Next moment a strong attraction like that which needles feel for magnets drew the children from the side of the Mer King. They shut their eyes, and when they opened them they were on dry land in a wood by a lake — and Francis had a ginger beer bottle in his hand. The King and Queen of the Under Folk must have said at once the charm to recall the children to earth.

"It works more slowly on land, the Astrologer said," Reuben remarked. "Before we drink and forget everything I want to tell you that I think you've all been real bricks to me. And if you don't mind, I'll take off these girls' things."

He did, appearing in shirt and knickerbockers.

"Good-bye," he said, shaking hands with everyone.

"But aren't you coming home with us?"

"No," he said, "the Astrologer told me the first man and woman I should see on land would be my long-lost Father and Mother, and I was to go straight to them with my little shirt and my little shoe that I've kept all this time, the ones that were mine when I was a stolen baby, and they'd know me and I should belong to them. But I hope we'll meet again some day. Good-bye, and thank you. It was ripping being General of the Sea Urchins."

With that they drank each a draught from the ginger beer bottle, and then, making haste to act before the oblivion-cup should blot out with other things the Astrologer's advice, Reuben went out of the wood into the sunshine and across a green turf. They saw him speak to a man and a woman in blue bathing dresses who seemed to have been swimming in the lake and now were resting on the marble steps that led down to it. He held out the little shirt and the little shoe, and they held *their* hands out to him. And as they turned the children saw that their faces were the faces of the King and Queen of the Under Folk, only now not sad any more, but radiant with happiness, because they had found their son again.

"Of course," said Francis, "there isn't any time in the other world. I expect they were swimming and just dived, and all that happened to them just in the minute they were underwater."

"And Reuben is really their long-lost heir?"

"They seemed to think so. I expect he's exactly like an ancestor or something, and you know how the Queen took to him from the first."

And then the oblivion-cup took effect and they forgot, and forgot forever, the wonderful world that they had known under seas, and Sabrina fair and the circus and the Mermaid whom they had rescued.

But Reuben, curiously enough, they did not forget: they went home to tea with a pleasant story for their father and mother of a Spangled Boy at the circus who had run away and found his father and mother.

And two days after a motor stopped at their gate and Reuben got out.

"I say," he said, "I've found my father and mother, and we've come to thank you for the plum pie and things. Did you ever get the plate and spoon out of the bush? Come and see my father and mother," he ended proudly.

The children went, and looked once more in the faces of the King and Queen of the Under Folk, but now they did not know those faces, which seemed to them only the faces of some very nice strangers.

"I think Reuben's jolly lucky, don't you?" said Mavis.

"Yes," said Bernard.

"So do I," said Cathay.

"I wish Aunt Enid had let me bring the aquarium," said Francis.

"Never mind," said Mavis, "it will be something to live for when we come back from the sea, and everything is beastly."

And it was.

THE END

The *Magic City*

by E. Nesbit
Illustrated by H.R. Millar

When young Philip Haldane builds a play city out of odds and ends from about the house, he never suspects that the city will magically come to life and that he and his new step-sister Lucy (who he bitterly resents) will be magically transported into it.

Now, caught inside the Magic City, they must try to save it by fulfilling an ancient prophesy. But determined to stop them is the mysterious Pretenderette who wishes to steal their glory and claim the title of the city's savior for herself.

The Magic City is an incredible place, filled with winged horses, talking animals, ancient buildings and magic islands.

How Philip and Lucy come to forge a friendship and work together to save the Magic City from impending disaster makes for a riveting, enchanting tale.

First published in 1910, *The Magic City* is one of Nesbit's best stories, filled with all the fantastic magic for which she is so justly famous. This edition contains her complete text and all the original 27 black-and-white pictures by H.R. Millar which graced the first edition.

Classic Tales
from
Books of Wonder®

The Sea Fairies
by L. Frank Baum
Illustrated by John R. Neill

Sky Island
by L. Frank Baum
Illustrated by John R. Neill

Dot and Tot of Merryland
by L. Frank Baum
Illustrated by Donald Abbott

The Enchanted Island of Yew
by L. Frank Baum
Illustrated by George O'Connor

Captain Salt in Oz
by Ruth Plumly Thompson
Illustrated by John R. Neill

Handy Mandy in Oz
by Ruth Plumly Thompson
Illustrated by John R. Neill

The Silver Princess in Oz
by Ruth Plumly Thompson
Illustrated by John R. Neill

Ozoplaning with the Wizard
by Ruth Plumly Thompson
Illustrated by John R. Neill

The Wonder City of Oz
Written and Illustrated by
John R. Neill

The Scalawagons of Oz
Written and Illustrated by
John R. Neill

Lucky Bucky in Oz
Written and Illustrated by
John R. Neill

The Runaway in Oz
by John R. Neill
Illustrated by Eric Shanower

The Magical Mimics in Oz
by Jack Snow
Illustrated by Frank Kramer

The Shaggy Man of Oz
by Jack Snow
Illustrated by Frank Kramer

Merry Go Round in Oz
by Eloise Jarvis McGraw and Lauren McGraw
Illustrated by Dick Martin

If you enjoy the Oz books and want to know more about Oz, you may be interested in **The Royal Club of Oz**. Devoted to America's favorite fairyland, it is a club for everyone who loves the Oz books. For free information, please send a first-class stamp to:

The Royal Club of Oz
P.O. Box 714
New York, New York 10011

Or call toll-free: (800) 207-6968

OZ
from
Emerald City Press™

Exciting Oz Stories
from a New Generation of Authors and Artists

How the Wizard Came to Oz
Written and Illustrated by
Donald Abbott

How the Wizard Saved Oz
Written and Illustrated by
Donald Abbott

The Magic Chest of Oz
Written and Illustrated by
Donald Abbott

The Speckled Rose of Oz
Written and Illustrated by
Donald Abbott

Father Goose in Oz
Written and Illustrated by
Donald Abbott

The Giant Garden of Oz
Written and Illustrated by
Eric Shanower

Masquerade in Oz
Written and Illustrated by
Bill Campbell and Irwin Terry

The Magic Dishpan of Oz
by Jeff Freedman
Illustrated by Denis McFarling

Nome King's Shadow in Oz
by Gilbert M. Sprague
Illustrated by Donald Abbott

The Patchwork Bride of Oz
by Gilbert M. Sprague
Illustrated by Denis McFarling

The Glass Cat of Oz
by David Hulan
Illustrated by George O'Connor

Christmas in Oz
by Robin Hess
Illustrated by Andrew Hess

Queen Ann in Oz
by Karyl Carlson & Eric Gjovaag
Illustrated by William Campbell and Irwin Terry

If you enjoy the Oz books and want to know more about Oz, you may be interested in **The Royal Club of Oz.** Devoted to America's favorite fairyland, it is a club for everyone who loves the Oz books. For free information, please send a first-class stamp to:

The Royal Club of Oz
P.O. Box 714
New York, New York 10011

Or call toll-free: (800) 207-6968